THE HISTORY OF THE VERTEBRATE

The right of Mar García Puig to be identified as Author of this Work has been asserted in accordance with the UK Copyright, Designs and Patents Act 1988

All rights reserved. No part of this book may be reproduced or transmitted in any form without the prior written consent of the publisher

La història dels vertebrats © 2023 by Mar García Puig
The English edition is published by arrangement with MB Agencia Literaria S.L
Translation copyright © Mara Faye Lethem 2026

Peninsula Press
400 Kingsland Road
E8 4AA
London
peninsulapress.co.uk

Typesetting by Geethik Technologies

Printed in Great Britain by CMP Books, Poole

The translation of this work has been supported by the Institut Ramon Llull
This book has been selected to receive financial assistance from English PEN's PEN Translates programme, supported by Arts Council England. English PEN exists to promote literature and our understanding of it, to uphold writers' freedoms around the world, to campaign against the persecution and imprisonment of writers for stating their views, and to promote the friendly co-operation of writers and the free exchange of ideas. www.englishpen.org

2 4 6 8 10 9 7 5 3 1

ISBN-13: 9781913512859

THE HISTORY OF THE VERTEBRATE

BY MAR GARCÍA PUIG

translated from Catalan by Mara Faye Lethem

PENINSULA PRESS, LONDON

*To my mother, Montserrat,
and my sister Georgina*

To Elisa and Milo, with many apologies

Her little bottom
sat in my palm, her chest contained
the puckered, moire sacs, and her neck –
I was afraid of her neck, once I almost
thought I heard it quietly snap,
I looked at her and she swivelled her slate
eyes and looked at me. It was in
my care, the creature of her spine, like the first
chordate, as if the history
of the vertebrate had been placed in my hands.

Sharon Olds
Her First Week

1

On 20 December 2015 I became a mother and I went mad. Close to midnight, in a white room in the Vall d'Hebron hospital in Barcelona, a head emerged from my body like a blaze in a bush. As I pushed, I thought I saw a dragon in the ceiling mouldings. When the baby burst into a sharp cry, already in foreign arms, the dragon flew out the window, its tail dragging the clear night's stars and dropping them to the floor with a thud. Before I realised it, distracted thinking who would clean up that stellar mess, I had my daughter on my chest, gelatine and miracle. 'Just one sec,' they told me, and as they snatched her away from me, they pressed hard on my belly. We weren't done yet. I continued conceiving that fire and saw a second head between my legs. I was surprised by another cry, which merged with the first and filtered with the din of a thousand waterfalls through the cracks in the delivery room. From above, they gave me my children, one on each side. And I wanted to count their fingers, and their toes. When I got to twenty, I kissed the pinkie on each of those paltry feet of burnished metal.

I blinked and suddenly they were no longer with me. I looked from side to side. Were they back inside my womb? Did they not like the world once they'd seen it? But beneath my breasts everything was empty. A doctor I'd never seen before approached me. The twins were on their way to the incubators, where machines would finish the task my womb hadn't. 'They have all their fingers and toes,' I informed them.

When the retinue of doctors disappeared, a reality I hadn't considered was revealed to me: I had given birth to a new world, because the one in which my children didn't exist had disappeared, and today everything was beginning.

The birth had opened the door that connects being and not-being, life and death, light and darkness, and I would never be able to close it.

In 1942, the poet Silvia Mistral, after giving birth to her daughter, wrote: 'I've returned from the dead and I didn't pray to God.' I didn't pray to God either, but I only half-returned from the dead.

The Ancient Greeks believed that our lives were in the hands of three dreaded and despised sisters, the Moirai. Even powerful Zeus was subject to their bidding. Daughters of the Night and infernal Darkness, these three withered women explain, from the echoes of history, that our lives hang by a thread. The youngest, Clotho, spins the thread of life; Lachesis measures it on the spindle, white for happy days and black for the unhappy ones; and finally Atropos, the most terrible of the sisters, cuts it with gleaming scissors, deciding the moment of our death. Greek brides, on their wedding day, try to placate them with locks of their luxuriant hair. Today, three asteroids that orbit between Mars and Jupiter bear the names of the three sisters. We don't see them but in the blackness of the universe they continue spinning.

I've managed to forget about the Moirai for most of my life. Recklessly, I offered up no locks of my hair. But amid the bedlam of birth, the three old women burst into the delivery room, shouting, and no one, except the new mother, saw them.

Men often express surprise over the pain we are able to tolerate during birth. But there is little to no talk of the path we set out upon, or the land of no return we see at the end of that path, where we and those we've given life to will become dust. Because, in conceiving the next generation, we as mothers confirm our own mortality, but above all we accept a risk of loss we can never elude. In the moment when the doctor placed my children on my chest for the first time, when what was not became blood, flesh, and bone, I knew that one day Atropos's scissors would cut the thread and the separation from my children would be final. And I couldn't accept that.

'O, let me not be mad, not mad, sweet heaven!' screamed King Lear, battered by the tempest, betrayal, and guilt in his inexorable road to madness. Like the raging sea, crowned with weeds and nettles, singing and wandering disoriented, a father becomes a child. Likewise, lugged on a stretcher to my hospital room, now a mother, I felt my wits deserting me. 'Keep me in temper. I would not be mad!' I scream in silence, but that starless night refused to listen to me.

As the euphoria of the births spread through our family and friends, another euphoria overtook the country. That same day, Spain was voting in the first elections that included a new party, one that strove to represent the common people, and the hope for change hovered. As night fell, when I was counting contractions in the dilation room, the country was counting ballots. And both counts converged into a new life for me, because one of those seats would end up being mine. The very day that my children were born, I became a member of Parliament.

Two years before I had received a diagnosis of infertility due to an endometriosis that was underestimated for too long. The fangs that had been chewing on my ovaries every twenty-eight days since adolescence weren't part of normal menstrual pain, as the doctors claimed, but one of the many female illnesses ignored by the cluster of men in white coats throughout history. One particularly arid autumn afternoon, on an infinitely typical day, a doctor called Bonaventura delivered a verdict much less favourable than his name: my fallopian tubes had to be removed. That was the end of any possibility of natural pregnancy, leaving only assisted conception. While Tomàs, the future father, and I held each other's hands, Dr Bonaventura showed us a laminated drawing of the female reproductive system with the tubes cut in half by some lines that looked to me like stakes. The state of the drawing, smudged and faded, spoke to how common the diagnosis was. But that didn't stop my tears from bubbling up. Sometime later, as I was researching my infertility, I found out that it was Gabriele Falloppio, the same man who lent us his name for my now useless tubes, who described for the first time the path that tears take from the tear duct before revealing themselves to the world. When Dr Bonaventura saw them, he told me not to be afraid. 'Nothing's impossible for science. You will conceive.'

Leaving his office, the crunch of the leaves beneath my feet sounded particularly hollow. The streets were suddenly dressed in mourning clothes. The ash covering the ground stuck to my heels and lightly stained the upholstery in the taxi that brought me to one of the political meetings that were part of my routine during those months. The great party of change, the one that wanted to transform how politics are done, had recently begun constructing itself, and from the very first day I knew I wanted to be a brick. During many months I juggled all sorts of tests to determine my options for becoming a mother with the laborious battle to ensure women had a voice in those long, exhausting debate sessions. I underwent a surgical operation that challenged my body's unproductiveness, while I was also, alongside many sisters, challenging a political drift that too often threatened to relegate us to the silence of history.

In the free time I had between work and medical appointments, I visited quite a few towns by train: meetings, gatherings, talks, presentations. And as I did, Job's words echoed inside me, his warning to those who deviated from the path of the Lord: they shall have no offspring or descendants, their memory will perish from the earth, they shall have no name in the land. Curved in my seat, looking out the window at the broken branches and wisps of hay that flit about the barren fields, I tried to think about the women who had walked these paths before. Just like the infertile, their memory had perished because they didn't have a public voice, battered by the also biblical scourge of inequality.

The first modern doctors elaborated a medical theory to continue battering them. The body is governed by a basic physiological law, they said, 'conservation of energy', according to which, humans have a limited amount of energy that our various organs compete for. Education, or any intellectual activity, could thus be physically dangerous for a woman, since it consumes too much energy and causes her uterus to atrophy. The intellect and public life are the enemies of procreation. The German mathematician Paul Julius Möbius wrote in the late nineteenth century: 'If we wish for a woman to fulfil the task of motherhood fully she cannot possess a masculine brain. If the feminine abilities were developed to the same degree as those of the male, her maternal organs would shrivel and we should have before us a repulsive and useless hybrid.' And even though today few people remember Möbius for those words, and even though that was centuries ago and some progress has been made, the conclusions he drew then continue to build walls.

This imperfect hybrid with dual ambitions I feared I had become placed all her faith in the words of Dr Bonaventura, who balanced out bad news with good. I could become a mother through in vitro fertilization, but my ovaries were trees with scant fruit and the task would be arduous. I then began the ovarian stimulation process: every night I pinched my belly and bravely pricked myself to inject the invigorating liquid into my body. I was barely able to offer up two miserly oocytes to the process and the possibilities of my getting pregnant were drastically reduced. But Dr Bonaventura assured me that everything would be fine. 'Cheer up, woman.' The whole thing had little to do with the magical remedies of medieval women, who lavished offerings on the fairies of the springs or subtly touched erect stones with phallic forms to honour their wombs. I was covered by science, and almost a hundred years since the first rabbit ovum was fertilized, the miracle of the test tube took root in my uterus.

One Monday morning I received a phone call with the verdict of the treatment that my blood had revealed: 'Don't drink wine. You're pregnant.'

Ever since I learned that my womb was an orchard, I was invaded by a sensation of euphoria coupled with panic. I knew that what was inside me would grow thanks to the nutrients my body gave it, but I was afraid that it would feed on my ghosts as well, the thistles and thorns I'd long feared were populating my uterus.

During the first ultrasound I couldn't look at the screen. What if it were all just a mirage? What if the palm trees and water they'd found just four weeks earlier had turned back into a desert? The father, on the other hand, stared intently, and I at him. And suddenly there was a beating. That of a flesh heart that had broken through the stone. 'Here's the first one,' said the doctor. And we both said, almost in unison: 'The first one?' 'Yes, you're pregnant with twins.' The only two oocytes I was capable of creating, that scarcity, was now abundance. Then we heard the second one, a tick tock that seemed to sound with a slightly different tone and, if not for my embarrassment, I would've joined in with its song. But my happiness was short-lived. 'This will be a high-risk pregnancy,' warned the doctor.

Nevertheless, in that new waiting period I took on surprising strength: I lifted my wings like an eagle, no amount of walking could tire me out. Anticipating the birth, I collected all the clothing and accoutrements necessary like someone gathering up sand by the sea. In order to know the gender of the foetus, according to Hippocrates, you have to look at the pregnant woman's skin; if it is in good condition, it will be a boy; if, on the other hand, it is haggard and ruined, it will be a girl. The Greek doctor hadn't foreseen cases like mine: I soon learned I was expecting a boy and a girl, and my facial skin gleamed strangely. In the sixteenth century, the French anatomist Jacobus Sylvius would continue the Hippocratic tradition by declaring that the womb, a small world in and of itself, is doubled, and that on the right side, where the blood has a better temperature, grows the more noble of the sexes, the male; the female has to make do with the sadder, poorer left side. But my body had decided it would do it the other way round. The girl, whom we would name Sara, was situated vertically on the right and her brother, David, was stretched out on the left side. According to Sylvius and his colleagues, that carried a risk: those virile and authoritarian women, the ones who had the gall to occupy the space reserved for men, had been mistakenly conceived on the right side of the uterus. And that also suggested that my son would be effeminate, delicate and easily breakable like the mother who would give birth to him.

It was already summer, which left me bathed in sweat, when I received an unexpected proposal: they wanted me to run in the upcoming parliamentary elections. I warned them of my situation, I told them that I was expecting not one but two babies, that it was very likely that the start of the term would coincide with the end of my pregnancy, but they remained firm in their offer: we want you there. And the hybrid said yes, through my lips. The primaries validated my desire, and I officially became a candidate for Barcelona.

I increased my political activity and paraded my awkward gravity through places I'd never set foot in before. As I took part for the first time in the creation of a political platform, my fingers were making two bodies, and the concreteness of the former clashed with the mysteriousness of the latter. I often wondered what I was making on any particular day. The Greek philosophers argued bitterly over what part of the body was created first: the Stoics maintained that everything was formed at the same time; Aristotle that, just like a boat's keel, it is the lumbar region that arises first; others gave priority to the heart or the head; but the theory that I found most convincing was the one that asserted everything began with the big toe. That was where I would begin constructing my edifice. And I wanted it round, chubby, and healthy.

The campaign began when I was already seven months into a difficult pregnancy, with haemorrhages that had brought me to the hospital several times, but by then they had calmed their ferocity. By that point I had already lost count of the kilos I'd gained, even though my doctor insisted on reminding me. Every millimetre of my body hurt. 'That's normal,' he would say, 'the body isn't designed for this.' My belly was gigantic, shockingly grandiloquent. According to a legend of the Pumi, a mountain people from Yunnan, China, in ancient times it was men who gave birth, but they carried the child in their calves. The problem was that the foetus didn't have room to grow there, and they gave birth to very small babies, toad-like creatures that never got larger than rabbits. They had to move the gestation function to women's wombs, which, as I was living proof of, had an unusual capacity to expand, which meant they could nurture strong humans, ready to win any war.

The campaign presentation event began in the evening and went on past midnight, with the traditional hanging of posters. I was set to be one of the speakers, and I'd prepared a short speech that spoke about the future I wanted for my children, as they'd suggested. The hall was filled with cameras, because the polls were already predicting we'd do very well, and I had never spoken in front of so many people. When my turn came, they helped me up to the stage. I was afraid of falling, of collapsing the wooden dais and starring in a gory tragic spectacle. But I gave my speech with nary a trace of hesitation, with a cogency and weight similar to that of my belly. That night I dreamt that I was giving birth. I birthed one child, then two, and as I was just about to stand up and put on my coat to leave, they shouted at me from within: 'Wait!' And then they began to emerge, one after the other, an army of babies that only ended with the scream that woke me up.

The Renaissance humanist Giovanni Pico della Mirandola gave testimony of a woman named Dorotea who gave birth, in two turns, to twenty children. An anatomy book recorded the singular case and depicted Dorotea pregnant with eleven foetuses, with a belly so enormous that, to keep it from dragging on the ground, she held it up with a long ribbon tied around her neck. During the campaign I became a modern Dorotea, a terracotta goddess with turgid breasts, hippopotamus body, and crocodile tail. No one looking at me could try to hide the bestiality of life with a story of a stork or a cabbage patch. Not even I had power over what was happening in my body, how could others possibly.

The belly bumps I used to clear a path for myself caused swoons of admiration, especially among older women, who – scandalised – would say: 'Oh, and how will you manage when you have to go to Madrid?' They knew full well how to formulate that question; after all, every mother throughout history has wondered that. How am I going to do it, millions have asked themselves, just like I asked myself in silence, even while seeming to have everything under control. And I had so little under control that a few days before the campaign ended my spine said there was no ribbon capable of bearing so much weight, my back gave out and my cervix began to dilate hastily. Despite the bedrest, the day of the elections, at six in the morning, my water broke. Even though the doctors tried all day long with various potions to keep me from going into premature labour, David and Sara had made a decision and no one was going to change their minds. At almost midnight, when the political commentators were already getting ready to return home, I gave birth to my fraternal twins.

In the nineteenth century, a lawmaker in Massachusetts proclaimed: 'Grant suffrage to women, and you will have to build insane asylums in every country, and establish a divorce court in every town. Women are too nervous and hysterical to enter into politics.' That man would've loved meeting me right after I gave birth, he would've so enjoyed seeing a politician and mother, on the cusp of her recognition and maturity, crumble. That distinguished man, dressed in an immaculate wool suit, watches me mockingly from a corner of the room I wake up in at dawn. Only a few hours have passed since I gave birth and, as I lift my eyelids, I'm surprised by the northern light coming in through the window.

Just then I'm crushed by the certainty that something is not right. Anything that happens in the next few seconds will prove it. I stand up and the room seems much bleaker than it did yesterday. It is austere and a curtain separates me from the bed of another woman whom I imagine sleeping placidly. I head to the bathroom. When I plop down heavily on the toilet, I feel a cold liquid running down my back. I look up and the false ceiling is completely dry. I pray that it's sweat. But with my hand I confirm that a spring is flowing from the back of my body. I am wearing a white nightgown of my grandmother's, with elaborate embroidery that is now soaked. I pounce on the light switch. A sulphurous luminosity floods the room. Horrified, I look at myself in the scuffed mirror, twisting to see my entire back. It looks like water, transparent liquid, but when I get closer I see a hint of increasing scarlet. With my pulse racing and the nightgown glued to my body, I return to my half of the room. The sun has drenched it in reddish rays that reveal walls covered in tattered paper. I slump onto the bed and everything is crimson stained: the once-white sheets, the whitewashed arches. I have no doubt that my body is bleeding out through the epidural puncture and flooding everything. Trembling, I manage to push the nurse call button. While I wait for her, I discover my body beneath the sheets. What had been common freckles are now filthy blotches that augur a grim future.

A thick fog smudges my memory of the next few hours. Over time, and thanks to my medical records, I've been able to reconstruct them. 'Patient in immediate postnatal warns of sensation of dampness around epidural puncture point. Dressing completely wet, upon removal I observe constant flow of transparent liquid. I notify gynaecology and anaesthesia,' noted the nurse who responded to my call.

The first doctor who comes to my room, a gynaecologist, examines me and finds an absence of pathology related to the puncture site. 'I respond to questions from the patient and family, trying to reassure them.' She explains that it is probably an insignificant incident, but she calls anaesthesiology to make sure and so we feel comforted. She confidently declares that I present none of the symptoms of complications linked to the epidural and that the liquid has already stopped flowing, but I'm not in the mood to trust her.

In a lapse of time during which the only movement I manage is shaking, an anaesthesiologist appears. 'Removal of epidural puncture site bandage, bandage is clean, slightly damp, show it to the patient.' She confirms that there are no worrisome symptoms, and as such recommends no treatment. But her notes focus on my state of mind: 'Patient displays fear and incoercible anxiety around complications and corollaries. I explain the situation, the therapeutic plan, and the possibilities of requesting assistance at any time, yet the fear she displays verbally and her disconsolate crying do not abate. Psychiatric consultation requested.'

Some hours pass, during which I refuse to budge from what has become the hospital bed of sadness. Tomàs, my mother, and my mother-in-law try to convince me that everything is fine. I only manage to shake my head. They ask me to go see my children, four floors below, but I am glued to that mattress tinged with a vermillion no one else can see. Every so often a nurse enters, removes my bandage and shows it to me, 'dry dressing', they repeatedly jot down in my record, followed by a psychological observation: 'distressed', 'obsessively asks about possible complications', 'anxious'. I insistently point to the wall, to a crack that travels in zigzag from the skirting board to the sky. It was barely visible when I awoke, but now its depth screams at me from the trembling glimmer that illuminates it. They repeat that it has been there forever and is nothing to worry about. But I fear that that deep crack will cause the collapse of the roof of this building filled with mothers and newborns.

Shortly after I refuse the lunch they bring me, the psychiatrist shows up. From the door, she asks Tomàs and my mother to leave the room. As she walks towards me her white coat shifts with a non-existent wind. She sits at the foot of my bed and before she can say a word, I erupt into deep sobs and tell her I'm going to die, and that I can't die, because I have two children. 'I can't die anymore,' I scream at her. 'I'm a mother.'

In the mid-nineteenth century, a tremendous number of women of very different positions and backgrounds began arriving, agitated and broken down, at British mental asylums. They were recently postnatal and suffering a series of nervous disorders, from violent deliriums to profound melancholy, for which the doctors had no precedents or answers. Something unknown, a never-before-seen madness, unleashed like a legion of demons poised to shred the sanctity of the Victorian home.

In 1864, a woman known by the initials B. C. was brought by her relatives to the Royal Edinburgh Asylum, the largest mental institution in Scotland. This married lady, naturally friendly and cheerful, a mother of five, had suffered a considerable haemorrhage seven days after giving birth. As soon as she lay down in bed, the haemorrhaging stopped, but the maniacal symptoms began. According to her medical file, when she was admitted she was so weak she was considered near death. At the same time she was terribly excitable, which caused great astonishment that someone so fragile could provoke a scandal of such magnitude. Her face was pale; her eyes, wild and staring. 'Her mania was of the wildest description, she incoherently raved that she had brought forth dogs instead of children, recognised old friends in the strangers now around her, cried that her food had been poisoned, pointed to imaginary objects.' At the entrance to the asylum, carved in stone, were Juvenal's famous words: 'Orandum est ut sit mens sana in corpore sano' (You should pray for a healthy mind in a healthy body). We don't know if prayer or psychiatry were able to do anything for her, because all trace of her was lost to history in the archives.

We do know what became of Eliza Gripps, who, at the other end of the island, in southern England, was admitted to the luxurious and exclusive Ticehurst House Hospital, four years earlier. She was brought there by her aunt after a complicated birth and scaring her entire family with a stubborn attitude and surprisingly filthy habits: 'Voiding her urine about the house and soiling her linen with faeces'. The notes of her admittance are a string of terrible ravings: 'She believes that there is still the same connection between herself & child as existed when in the womb, that he is influenced by her own state of health, by the food she takes, & by the action of her own bodily functions. For instance if the child is away from her she will eat immoderately, that he may be supported through her during his absence – she also believes that when obeying the call of nature she is passing out her own & the child's life & consequently restrains the action of the bowels as long as she possibly can do so – She states that her attendants and servants have the power of taking her mind from her, that they can produce internal pain with her at pleasure that they are the cause of her hair falling off, of weakness in her back, deformity of her toes'.

Some months later, Eliza's state of mind stabilised, she was more docile and chatted with the other ladies, spent her time sewing and playing chess, but she continued to be deeply distressed by the separation from her son and she would secretly save food for him. Over time, those moods would alternate with manic episodes where she became violent, refused food and tried to hold in her faeces. She always showed a heartrending affection for her son, talked about him constantly and expressed a desire to return home to take care of him. One New Year's Eve she refused to go to bed, convinced that 'her carriage was coming to take her home to her child'. She stayed up all night but, from her admittance to her death nine years later in the same asylum, she never saw him again.

Not all the stories had a tragic end. Margaret Steele's offers a wisp of hope. She was taken to the Edinburgh asylum in 1855 in a terrible state twelve weeks after her third child was born. She was screaming that the devil had taken her children and that her soul was lost. She paced through the hallway wringing her hands and crying. She refused to eat. She is 'victim of most unhappy delusions she fancies that the meat she eats is composed of the bodies of her murdered children'. She was treated with morphine and force-fed beef broth. Gradually she improved and a year later they decided to bring her children to visit her. To the astonishment of the hospital staff and her husband, when Margaret saw them she denied they were her children, who she claimed amid sobs had been murdered. 'Oh you have killed my bonnie bairns,' she screamed. It would be another year before she was able to see them 'without any adverse affects' and finally return home happily.

The most important woman in England, the mother of the United Kingdom, Queen Victoria herself, succumbed to nervous disorders associated with childbirth. The Victorian doctors made mention of this, concerned how her example might affect other women. After the birth of her second child, she suffered an episode of anguish and despondency about which the personal secretary to Prince Albert wrote: the queen was in extremely low spirits, 'I should say that Her Majesty interests herself less and less about politics'. Her emotional malaise was never extreme, surely muffled by her wealth and rank. But the leader of the largest empire in history, revered, feared, and adored throughout the world, would never forget how motherhood had reduced her to this submissive, suffering state. In a letter to her daughter, following the birth of her grandson, she wrote about the royal princess' husband: 'I hope Fritz is duly shocked by your sufferings, for those very selfish men would not bear for a minute what we poor slaves have to endure'.

'Puerperal insanity', 'mania lactea', 'amentia' and 'dreamlike delirium'. Various terms were used to try to circumscribe this new phenomenon: a scandalous ailment, to which the emerging fields of obstetrics and psychiatry devoted titanic efforts. Robert Gooch, a British obstetrician, was the first to write about it, in 1820, in his influential treatise *Observations on Puerperal Insanity*: 'When puerperal mania does take place, the patient swears, bellows, recites poetry, talks bawdy, and kicks up such a row that there is the devil to pay in the house.'

Puerperal insanity defied the hegemony of domestic ideology. Women were abandoning their tasks, challenging their husbands, breaking plates, and tearing clothes; violent and dirty, they wandered the streets and showed themselves to be sexually shameless. They suffered explosions of rage, but were also capable of becoming lost in thought, like statues petrified by their own guilt. Then no object, as beautiful as it might be, awakened their senses, no music managed to rekindle them. What was most surprising and the focus of much study was the fierce mania; however, the doctors observed that serpentine, treacherous melancholy was harder to cure.

The new mothers were the living proof of the failure of the model of the Victorian woman, a distorted spectre of themselves. The medical staff extracted the milk from their breasts, fed them like babies with spoons and catheters, and in their medical records they referred to them as if they were in a state of permanent childish obstinacy. They no longer retained any of that innate talent all mothers should possess for making their home a haven of peace and morality.

The same England that saw the growth of enormous factories and cities overflowing with modernity, the same

England that designed the great transatlantic ships and the trains that were the epitome of progress, put limits on women by building a culture of two spheres, that kept wives locked at home while men comfortably occupied public space. The tyrannical clichés of motherhood, hidden beneath the idea of the 'angel in the house', that pure, good, and self-sacrificing being, were the necessary cement. The birthplace of modern capitalism was also the birthplace of the prototype of the good mother, whose sinister shadow still hangs over the delivery rooms of the entire Western world.

A change in the way of controlling women had been brewing since the late eighteenth century: from a religious logic it shifted to a biomedical one, in which the old cassocks were swapped out for stethoscopes. Like Yahweh to Eve, the new medical elite told women it was their duty to bring forth children in pain, and that desire for and submission to their husbands was in their biology. But they weren't allowed to forget they'd been born from a rib, a curved, twisted, and imperfect bone, and that everything about them was weakness. And the anatomists offered proof of that. According to them, the entire female body was designed for motherhood, and everything about it was fragility. Their bones were smaller and softer than men's, and their ribcage, narrower. Their pelvis, wide and curved to contain a foetus, provoked an obliquity in the femurs that would make walking difficult, because their knees knocked together. Their hips swung to find the centre of gravity, their gait was hesitant and uncertain. Their spongy damp tissues and their flaccid frail muscles expanded to wrap the baby. Their brains were small. Their thin, fragile skin housed many branches of blood vessels and nerves, conferring them with exquisite sensitivity. Crushed beneath the obligation of perpetuating the species and hammered with empirical evidence that disorder and failure was in her nature, the Victorian wife undertook motherhood with an atrocious uncertainty.

The alienists who treated puerperal insanity faced an enormous challenge: they were not only trying to cure a woman, but trying to cure a family, to have the deranged woman return to her role as mother and wife. The foundations of a way of organising the world were in their hands. Waves of insanity threatened to make the sluggish waters of Victorian society overflow their banks, and the alienists were charged with keeping them in their channel. But who can hold the ocean in a paper cup?

2

In 1828, British alienist George Man Burrows described what would happen the day after I gave birth on the fourth floor of a maternity ward in Barcelona in the twenty-first century: 'Fondly anticipating the joy, perhaps of a first-born, a beloved wife patiently submits to all the inconveniences and restraints of pregnancy, however irksome, and the pains and dangers of labour, however great. The affectionate husband and relatives await with deep and anxious expectation the event; and at length, when the joyful period arrives, and the happiness of all is completed by a safe delivery, – how dreadfully is the scene reversed, when the happy mother suddenly displays symptoms of delirium!'

The devil has free reign in my hospital room and, according to my medical records, no medical authority is capable of exorcising him. Showing me the completely dry bandage every so often does no good. 'The patient is vigilant, conscious and focused, but with obsessive hypochondriacal thoughts. High anxiety.' Victorian psychiatrists believed these types of states were influenced by a large accumulation of blood in the head, and they would shave women's heads and apply cold to their skulls to lessen the heat and send the blood flow to other parts of their bodies. But it was also in nineteenth-century England that 'moral treatment' took hold, promoted at the York Retreat by Quaker tea merchant William Tuke. In that idyllic brick building with a slate roof, surrounded by bucolic pastures and gardens, they got rid of the chains and prohibited any form of violence. Because insanity was no longer a loss of reason with fantastical tinges, but a brutally human experience, a shift from socially accepted behaviour, and so the asylum's mission was not to imprison lunatics but domesticate them. In order to do so, all efforts were placed into re-educating their dirty, obscene habits, their unproductivity and laziness, their lack of self-control and modesty. These asylums seemed more like pre-schools than dark dungeons, and they were organised using a respectable family as the model: the head alienist and his wife carried out the roles of father and mother, the nurses were older sisters and the patients were the children who needed to be educated. Embroidery, cooking, and laundry chores were the cornerstones of restoring women to proper decorum and piety.

For me there is no time for cross-stitch, and science today swears that what regulates the mood in our brains is not an accumulation of blood but rather a series of neurotransmitters with hypnotic names. Furthermore, in my case, the brutal drop in what are called placental hormones after birth could also be causing my discomfort. 'Treatment with paroxetine recommended', the psychiatrist writes firmly on my medical record.

Paroxetine is a second-generation anti-depressant, a direct descendant of the first anti-depressant, isoniazid, a medication originally used to treat tuberculosis, whose effects against depression were discovered by chance. In 1952, at the Sea View Hospital of New York, several tuberculous patients treated with the drug began to display an unusual vitality and euphoria, to the surprise of the medical staff and journalists who crowded around to attest to it. A newspaper photograph shows the effects after one year. In it several residents seem to be at a party filled with optimism. The caption reads: 'A few months ago, the only sound here was the sound of victims of tuberculosis, coughing up their lives.' Another periodical claimed the patients were 'dancing in the halls tho' there were holes in their lungs.'

The philosopher Michel Foucault wrote that Victorian psychiatric treatments formed a 'gigantic moral prison'. I don't know whether the drug they are going to give me will be a cell or wings, but clearly psychiatric drugs have revolutionised our world. The consumption of anti-depressants is today so exorbitant that it is believed they are even affecting ecosystems. Because the amounts we excrete are beginning to filter into the environment. According to a recent study, freshwater crabs exposed to anti-depressant pollution are bolder and more reckless: they emerge more quickly from their dens, fearlessly show their claws to predators, and lose all notion of time when they are searching for food. They are easier prey but die sated, I imagine, although the study doesn't mention anything about that.

In my case, they are hoping this prescription provokes in me the bold recklessness to forget about the sickle hanging over me, go down to the newborn ward and look at my children, ignoring the obsessive voice that keeps reminding me that one day I won't ever be able to see them again. In short, to get me dancing while I cough up my lungs filled with holes. But to my anguish, the iron is straw and the bronze, rotted wood.

My medical record states that it is six pm on the dot when I leave my room and head to the newborn section. With trembling steps, I walk through dusky, intricate hallways whose windows seem to be niches of pure darkness. When I open that door that weighs centuries and in whose creaking I think I can hear the lamentations of a thousand mothers, a room filled with dozens of monitors opens out before me. I imagine a short circuit. A doctor tripping. The lives hanging by the thread of a cord. And the shadow of death that accompanies me projects over the entire room.

The nurses look at me. Surely they are making conjectures about the time of day and my previous absence. The nightgown the hospital lent me drags on the floor; the stains on the one I'd brought couldn't be cleaned with all the bleach in the world. I'm embarrassed by my corpse-like appearance, my eyes bloodshot from constant sobbing, my hand that refuses to stop touching my back to check the state of my bandage. Tomàs looks at me from a shabby armchair located between two cribs and makes a gesture with both arms. There they are, woman, your children.

I walk towards them and the light radiating from the twins dazzles me. Everything seems to fade to black, except for that sunny gleam in the dog days of summer that now illuminates me. When my eyes get used to it, I see two tiny beings, mustard seeds, who more than children look like fish in a thousand reddish tones, as if not fully fleshed out, who flail their extremities around trying to swim in non-existent water. I approach them to make sure that they are breathing, even if it's through their gills.

David looks more premature, which paradoxically means he looks more like an old man. Sara seems more completed, with an upturned nose that points at the sky. Her light blue eyes contrast with David's dark black ones, which gleam like two sword blades. Purple rivers run through their skin. Their toothless gums are intensely crimson. Their cheeks are bits of pomegranate, the scant hair that crowns their heads, golden wool. Those tiny, perfectly round knees glow like a bale of wheat beneath the morning rays. I have the rainbow before me and all I can think about is death.

I feel as if I'm dressed in worms, while they wear pure white robes that give off the scent of fresh fields. But what is covering them is insufficient. I'd like to put them in an armour of scales to protect them from any anomaly to the constant sound of their vitals, from any fickleness in those tubes that threaten to never let them go.

The nurse speaks to me. She tells me they are doing fine, that the paediatrician will come down to talk to me as she already has with their father. And she repeats what he's already told me, that they just need help regulating their temperature, that for the moment they don't need a feeding tube, and that I can nurse them. With a leaden voice that shocks me, I tell her I don't think I have any milk, not a single drop.

She encourages me to hold them. And I do. My first task as a mother consists of changing a nappy. The nurse comes over to show me how to do it and then says, 'They've already passed the meconium.' The word reverberates in my head. For days, months. Six years later it still haunts me.

In his *Historia Animalium*, Aristotle writes that the Greek women were already using that term to refer to newborn's first faeces. The word comes from the Greek *mēkōnion*, a diminutive of 'poppy' that alludes to the dark juice of that flower. The meconium is that same colour, like tar, viscous and gluey. It is made up of the materials ingested during the time the baby spends in utero: intestinal epithelial cells, lanugo, mucus, amniotic fluid, bile, and water. It is apparently repulsive but somehow comprises the last observable vestige of the babies' presence inside me. And I missed it. Not having seen the meconium is also proof of an undeniable reality: I wasn't with my children during their first hours of life. Because I was mad, wrestling with Lucifer, four floors above them. And then a slight breeze seems to pick up, turning into a wind that smacks my cheeks with the weight of history.

The face of a mother is the face of the world. That is the solid castle psychology has built on seemingly scientific pillars since the mid-twentieth century. When David and Sara look at me they don't see my long, now gaunt face. They see the surface of the universe, and where panic is unleashed: 'If the nursling does not see the maternal gaze directed towards him, but instead glimpses it as something rigid, dead, cold, absent, then the world will also seem closed, impenetrable, and distant.'

According to prominent psychoanalyst Massimo Recalcati, I was conferring a dead world to my children. And not only that, because Recalcati states that, just like nesting dolls, a mother's face contains her own mother's face. In my case, the weight falls not only on me but also on my mother and the limitations of an education during the dictatorship, on my grandmothers and their hardships during the war, and on their mothers and their rural struggles, and so on in an endless succession that includes every mother in history. Any stain, any deficit in any of us, and all is lost.

A pregnant woman visits a famous psychoanalyst for advice on how to raise her baby so he'll be happy. The doctor responds, 'Come back in four years and I'll tell you everything you did wrong.' If I were the mother in this joke, I wouldn't even have to wait that long.

In the twentieth century, when the world felt a decrease in the panic over childhood mortality, a new threat for fragile babies arrived: their mothers' unconscious, their libido, narcissism, their compulsions, emotions, fears, obsessions. The casuistry is limitless, but it always contains the words 'too much'.

These new warnings from psychology followed in the footsteps of the antiquated religious and anatomical theories. It was, in part, an explosion of optimism, of love of children, a desire to make a better world. But it is hard to not suspect that the same familiar metal was beneath that gold plating. Because every time the experts focus on the psyche of children, their instinct is to judge mothers and find fault with them. And their verdicts suggest that it is precisely the behaviour of unconventional mothers that is the main source of childhood damage.

One December morning in 1868, Jane Duncanson, a month after giving birth to her third child, decided to shut her mouth forever and never eat again. Faced with her suicidal obstinacy, her family members took her to the Edinburgh asylum. There they told the doctors that because of a poorly cured cold, she had developed an abscess in her breast that prevented her from breastfeeding her son, who nonetheless was perfectly fine. 'I killed my son,' she was screaming, unconsolably, to the alienist.

Like Jane, many patients arrived at the Victorian madhouses convinced they had committed horrific crimes. Most frequently they lamented having harmed their children, so they refused to look at them or go near them. They didn't want to see the atrocities they had wrought. Some of them believed they had already been judged and condemned, and that instead of a madhouse they were living in a vast prison. But that wasn't enough. They knew they could never pay for their terrible crimes. Single mothers raved about nonexistent husbands or imminent weddings that no one had any inkling of. Many of them made the Prince of Wales, the symbol of masculinity par excellence, the protagonist of their deliriums, and they accused him of either being the heartless father of their child and now wanting to wash his hands of the whole mess, or of being their fiancé and saviour, about to sweep in and take them to the palace.

The day after I went mad, the gynaecologist came to visit me again. She gave me a routine checkup that included squeezing my breasts to see if liquid emerged from the nipples. The medical record registers that we struck gold: 'Breast appearance normal. Bilateral colostrum.' The doctor suggests I try to extract milk with a device that is in the adjoining room, since it's likely the babies won't yet be able to latch on and suck.

The contraption designed to milk my breasts seems archaic. But I'm willing to do anything to give my children those defences that will be their armour. William Buchan, author of nineteenth-century best-selling medical books, assured that, if all women nursed our children with massive amounts of milk, we could put an end to the cruel ravages of death in the first years of life: 'Every child, invigorated by his mother's milk, would, like young Hercules, have force sufficient to strangle in his cradle any serpents that might assail him.' I want that for my children; I long to imbue them with the power to crush the reptiles snaking through the air holes in their incubators, but after a long time milking myself, I've barely covered the bottom of the bottle. The goddess Hera spilled the abundance from her breasts to create the Milky Way; mine, however, can only be seen through a magnifying glass.

I go down to the neonatal ward and with my gaze on the floor I show the nurses that scarcity. 'Nothing goes to waste around here,' they encourage me. They put it in a syringe, and they invite me to pick up one of my babies and give it to them. When I do, their lips become eager circles gripping the stem but, in less than a second, they've devoured it. And there's nothing left for the other one. I spend the rest of the day between the lactation room and the neonatal ward, where I study every movement of my children. My previous silence now becomes a constant question that the nurses and doctors who come in and out don't always have an answer for. The bandage is dry, but the unpredictable could flood the world.

Throughout history there have been many lunatics who, like Atlas, believed they carried the world on their shoulders. The Byzantine doctor Alexander of Tralles documented the case of a woman who claimed to sustain the entire universe with her thumb. She would cry in fear that if she bent it even just a little, everything would perish. These types of thoughts, doctors agreed, were due to the heaviness of melancholy, which when oppressing the brain provoked the feeling that one is bearing a great physical burden. Another factor was the weakness of the mad, for whom all weight was too much.

That night I tell Tomàs we need to talk. I want to tell him that I am carrying the world in my hands, even though he can't see it, that life and death are as close as a dry nipple, a wet bandage, an overheating cord. I know that the psychiatrist has spoken with him, that she told him that what's happening to me can happen to new mothers, that he shouldn't pressure me, that I'll get better. But he remains in his glacier.

We leave the room and take a walk. The maternity building at the Vall d'Hebron hospital is some sort of round tower, and we soon begin to walk in silent circles. There seem to be torches hung on the walls, giving off a faint light, but it doesn't matter, we barely look at each other. At any moment a bat or a scorpion could come out of some nook, and even that couldn't increase my distress.

The first sanatorium in continental Europe devoted exclusively to the crazy was opened in Vienna in 1784. It was a circular stone tower called Narrenturm, the Tower of Fools. Despite its stern appearance, according to psychiatric history it was one of the first places where patients were treated with a certain humaneness. Only those considered dangerous were tied up, and the rest were allowed to stroll on each of its five stories. They wandered in circles, like Tomàs and I right now, like the conversation we're having, like madness itself. We sit down on some stairs. 'There are two babies who need you,' he says to me. Tomàs's tears and mine become part of this immense circular ceremony that more and more objects are orbiting around in. And there is no way out.

The Tower of Fools was built under Joseph II, Emperor of the Holy Roman (Germanic) Empire. There are many legends about his relationship to Freemasonry and other secret societies, some of which are linked to the Tower. Supposedly the numbers related to the tower's design are occult messages. For example, each floor had twenty-eight rooms that housed the same number of lunatics, to emulate the days of the lunar cycle. On the top floor of the Tower, there was a small octagonal room where purportedly Joseph II would spend hours, although no one knows exactly what he was doing there. One theory is that the emperor believed that lunatics are endowed with an extremely powerful energy, so much that they were unable to hold onto it. The energy would seep upwards to the top of the Tower, where the emperor could absorb it.

Now I think, where is my energy? The still teenage energy with which I desired Tomàs when I would see him at the arthouse cinema, at barely nineteen years old. That energy with which I flipped convention on its head and declared that I liked him when I ran into him on Midsummer's Eve, already in my thirties. That energy with which we fell in love and moved in together despite our constantly colliding temperaments. That energy that kept us together for years against all prognoses, including our own. That energy with which we decided to become parents and we tackled infertility and my anxiety, which had already shown its face during the sweet waiting period. Now that our children are here, now that the doctors are saying that everything is fine, now an emperor shows up and takes that energy from me.

I visited the Narrenturm one summer I spent in Vienna studying German. It currently houses the Pathologisches-Anatomisches Bundesmuseum. The guided tour was led by medical students in white coats, who lead visitors through the old rooms for the crazy folk, now filled with human bodies and parts with anomalies and deformities preserved in formaldehyde. I particularly remember the body of a child inside a jar. The student told us he suffered a dermatological disorder called ichthyosis, in which the skin cells accumulate into scales. He looked like a fish.

In the days that follow I look at my children and they seem like unexplored territory. I map them in search of dragons. In my mind are draughtman's squares and triangles, in a never-ending cartographic geometry. Nothing sates my thirst for verification. Looking at them floods me with equal parts love and terror, and I gradually discover that they are two sides of the same existential coin. I fear death so much because I suddenly value life more than I ever had before.

During my first days as a mother, the hooded one with a scythe not only never leaves my side, but I occasionally catch him whistling around the cradles of my babies.

There is a fifteenth-century engraving in which Death appears beside a basket where a child sleeps. His mother seems a bit sceptical, but Death shows her his authorisation: a sealed parchment that was handed to him by God himself, the God of the epidemics that devastated medieval Europe. In the text that accompanies it, the mother laments:

Ay, my child is going to die,
the very apple of my eye.
Yet I cannot save him, do what I might,
death is stronger than darkest night.

And yet, the dozens of children who are growing in the neonatal ward are proof of just the opposite. Somehow, they are plump and full of life. The walls are decorated with letters and drawings from former patients, some with before and after photos that tempt one to believe in miracles: a baby that barely filled a palm now poses with a football and the jersey of his favourite team; another before picture shows a baby with an oval-shaped head and covered in thousands of tubes, who now looks at the camera impishly through thick glasses. And what they are saying is exactly what the paediatrician says when I explain all my fears about my children's health: 'Relax, life finds a way.'

But the fear doesn't fade. Even the strongest mother, the one on the firmest ground, has sometimes felt fear for her children. The writer Joan Didion confesses in a book devoted to her daughter Quintana: 'Once she was born I was never not afraid.' And her fears are unremitting: 'I was afraid of swimming pools, high-tension wires, lye under the sink, aspirin in the medicine cabinet, The Broken Man himself. I was afraid of rattlesnakes, riptides, landslides, strangers who appeared at the door, unexplained fevers, elevators without operators and empty hotel corridors.'

Maternal fear is a ferocious force that shaped our world. The very underpinnings of our civilisation, our foundational myths, are based in the pain of mothers. A stroll through Madrid's Museo Nacional Arqueológico, which I will visit several times in my new phase, is enough to comprehend that, on those December and January days when my children are in the hospital, night falls early and the ground is barren precisely because of a mother's grief. In the room devoted to red Greek ceramics, just at the end, a hydria depicts a mother and daughter, Demeter and Persephone, who together give the hero Triptolemus the art of agriculture and make the earth a fertile paradise. But it was not always thus. There was a time when the sobbing of Demeter, goddess of the harvest and fertility, turned the world into a wasteland.

One afternoon, as she was playing and gathering flowers with the daughters of Oceanus, Demeter's daughter was abducted by her uncle Hades. Just as she was picking a narcissus flower, the earth opened up and Hades carried her off to the underworld to be his queen. As she disappeared into the abyss, Persephone's shrill screams echoed in the mountaintops. Her mother, hearing her cries, ripped apart the band adorning her hair, threw a dark cloak over her shoulders and set off like a bird of prey in search of her daughter. During the next nine days and nine nights she wandered with flaming torches in her hands. Without eating, without drinking, without washing, without dressing up, she constantly repeated Persephone's name but could not find her. Disguised as an old woman, she went to live with the humans in Eleusis, abandoning all hope. But there young Triptolemus informed her what had befallen her daughter. Enraged, the goddess forbade the trees from bearing fruit and the seeds from prospering. That year, the world suffered a fatal famine and the gods were deprived of their offerings. In the face of this disaster, Zeus intervened: 'You can recover your daughter, as long as she has not tasted the food of the dead.' As it turned out, Persephone had eaten seven pomegranate seeds. Demeter refused to lift the curse she had cast on the earth. Finally, the gods came to an agreement: Persephone would spend a third of the year below in the nebulous darkness of Hades, the winter months when nothing is fecund. The rest of the year, when the world turns green again, she would spend alongside her mother.

And now, in the centre of Madrid, behind glass, Demeter and Persephone thank Triptolemus for helping bring about their reunion, and they gift him a large winged chariot drawn by a dragon with which to plant seeds from the air across the planet, while mother and daughter wash their hands of arduous human labours and enjoy their time together.

3

In the hours I spend surrounded by incubators, the country is undergoing frenetic political activity. The elections haven't brought change, but for the first time a party that rejects bipartisanship and has a desire to govern, a party of the common people, bursts into the Parliament and could be fundamental to the formation of the new government. The offices of the capital are bustling with negotiations, but for the moment the pact doesn't seem possible. While the bigwigs in Madrid negotiate power, I try to negotiate with death and knead bread dough.

On 13 January 2016, the XI Spanish Parliament is established, and I have to be sworn in as a member of the House of Commons. I go to Madrid with a breast pump and tonnes of figures I've retained from the hospital: the babies' weight, oxygen saturation, temperature, pulse. But, above all, I go with a complete database of all the features of their faces. I must memorise them, not forget them for even a second, because otherwise I worry they will vanish like the morning fog. I know there is a team of nurses and doctors with years of experience, a father tethered to those cribs. But I also know that, according to a study from some university somewhere in the world, being separated from their mother for three hours a day during their first weeks of life has lasting effects on children's brain circuitry, cognition, and behaviour. And I didn't even see their meconium.

I travel at dawn on a winged train that crosses a desert. When I arrive at the Parliament I don't see any television cameras or curious onlookers. What captures my gaze are the two imposing lions on either side of the columned portico, flanking the solemn steps, custodians of the kingdom of power. Symbols of national pride, they were commissioned in the nineteenth century from the sculptor Ponciano Ponzano, who spent countless hours in the Cabinet of Osteology in the Jardin des Plantes in Paris studying the animal's morphology so he could imbue the statues with a naturalism capable of reflecting its ferocity. Everything about them is strong, even the material, bronze from cannons seized from the defeated in the Battle of Wad-Ras. But beneath that strong appearance, those lions hide the weakness of insanity.

Legend has it that they represent Atalanta and Hippomenes. Atalanta was a beautiful Greek heroine who spent her time hunting and had no interest in marriage. Since she could run extremely fast, in order to get rid of her suitors, she would challenge them to a race. If any man could beat her, he would win her as his wife; all who lost would die. Young Hippomenes fell hopelessly in love with her and begged Aphrodite, the goddess of love, to help him. She gave him three golden apples, which Hippomenes threw during the race to distract Atalanta and win. But when Hippomenes had got what he wanted, he forgot about Aphrodite. He didn't even thank her or bring incense to her altar. The goddess was enraged and decided to take revenge: while the couple were in a temple dedicated to Cybele, Aphrodite drove them mad with lust and they sated their desire in that sacred place. Then, the couple began to sprout ginger hair, their fingers became claws, paws grew from their shoulders, and a tail finally sealed their animal transformation. Cybele's rage had turned them into lions.

Another famous building, in this case the antithesis of reason, was also flanked by two lunatics. Bedlam was, since its creation in the Middle Ages on the outskirts of London, the gloomy symbol of all asylums, the Bastille of psychiatric institutions. It was rightly deemed a dog kennel for the demented due to its inhumane and brutal treatment. Throughout its history, its raving, filthy, tied-up patients were exhibited for the amusement of the upper classes, who would spend their leisurely afternoons visiting its cells. When they arrived, two naked stone men would give them a sinister welcome.

Sculpted by Caius Gabriel Cibber, those two immense figures above the main gate represented Melancholy Madness and Raving Madness. The former seems to gaze into the world's vacuousness, the latter shows us a slice of hell: chained, his mouth half-open, he twists his neck and hands.

But at the cusp of the Victorian era, the statues were removed from the facade. In those years, the dialectic of reason and its absence was resolved as an opposition between the two sexes, and the symbolic gender of the mad shifted from male to female. The myth of the irrational woman flowed through the ideology of the two spheres, and those two madmen were hidden from public view inside a room of the institution, behind heavy drapery.

A few years ago, the virility of the two mad lions of the Spanish Parliament was called into question. If two men cannot welcome people into the temple of lunacy, a lion without testicles cannot flank the seat of power. A television channel specialising in history denounced the fact that one of the lions was neutered. It seems they ran out of the enemy bronze during the casting, and they decided to renounce the least visible part of the animal. The channel campaigned for those in charge of the Parliament's artistic patrimony to correct the flagrant defect. But the lion remains mad and castrated. Like me. Nonetheless, I am about to occupy a parliamentary seat.

From the moment I enter the chamber, the light from above falls on me like a fishing net. I shrug it off and lift my eyes. The magnificence of the room crushes me. Paintings in the Renaissance style, mahogany furnishings, bronze lamps, polychromatic marbles, golden railings, and Baroque tapestries, carpeted floors that hush my footsteps. There is some sort of horror vacui that incessantly transports me to the austerity of the four bars of the crib where my children sleep.

The House of Commons is made up of three hundred and fifty members. According to the Ministry of Health, in Spain one in ten people has a mental health issue. If the House of Commons is representative of the popular sovereignty, it doesn't seem ridiculous to think that it's representative in every way. So, for a simple rule of three, today, here, thirty-five people who've at some point had an intimate relationship with melancholy are about to be sworn in.

During this plenary session, the members of the bureau, the body that presides over the chamber, will be chosen. Each of the representatives will have to walk, several times, from our seats elevated in the shape of an amphitheatre, over to a wooden box located on a platform to cast our votes with paper ballots, and later we will each, one by one, promise to fulfil our post. It is a session filled with waiting, where actual political work is in short supply and one's mind is prone to wandering through the benches. And I can't stop scrutinising the features of my new colleagues in search of something that reveals their pain. How many of them have suffered an agonising loss, how many an insurmountable heartbreak? How many of them have been brought to the edge of madness by that suffering? And how many, without having endured a great catastrophe, have gone mad at the fear of one? It's impossible that all this apparent rectitude is real, it's impossible that there has never been a cry of anguish behind so much solemnity. But good politics are ruled by reason, banishing emotion, and everyone here seems to know that. And if we forget, the decor surrounding us is there to remind us. In the roof's dome, beside the skylight, surrounded by scrolls and grotesques, some paintings in Raphael's style allegorically represent the cardinal virtues that every MP must possess: Prudence and Justice on one side, Temperance and Strength on the other. They are lovely, serene women. Young. With immaculate complexions.

My breasts hurt with all the accumulated milk. I feel like I might burst at any moment, becoming viscous liquid that stains the carpet. Ancient doctors considered the female body a 'half-baked' version of the male. Because women had gestated on the left side of the uterus and received less warmth, we wouldn't be able to process waste well, so we would have to eliminate it in the form of menstruation or milk. That is why, where men are dry, we are damp; where they are rock, we are sponge. Furthermore, as Plato reasoned, the uterus, indisputable centre of our being, is in the belly, far from the rational soul and from noble thought. As such, where men are discernment, we are emotion. It seems hard to imagine today that I – pure feeling and liquid – will live up to this ornamental setting. So, every once in a while, I go to the toilet and pull out a device to empty my breasts and make it seem, for a bit longer, that I am fully baked.

However, there is no device capable of that. Nor would it work for me to go back home and accept my incapacity. Because this projection of the female body as a walking emotion doesn't settle for merely excluding women, its oversized ambition hides beneath a thousand layers of reason the fact that politics is also impregnated with emotion. Over time I will learn that what is relegated to the margins is at the very centre of thought, in this solemn chamber as well. All the political rationality of imposing MPs, loquacious spokespersons, and powerful ministers is also bathed in feeling. Far from the hierarchies and antagonisms that are so in vogue within these walls, rational thought is also emotional. Our own political awakenings are marked by the sadness and joy, admiration and fondness, the outrage that led us to the convictions we now hold. In fact, it was my late father who led me to this chamber, the person who first taught me about politics, the man who told me how the poverty of his ancestors led them to madness, the person who left too soon and whom I try to keep alive by running for office. I would like to go up to each member of Congress, even those who are furthest from me ideologically, and ask them what dead person is with them today.

When the session ends, we take the obligatory photo with the lions. We lift our arms, shout yes we can. I see the faces of my children in the neonatal ward and I realise that both here and there I am a prisoner of hope.

One of the rites of passage of every MP is the taking of the photograph that will appear in their file, available to all through the official website. Since I couldn't get to Madrid earlier, the photographer will take mine after the plenary session. I am wearing a black dress with grey pinstripes and a bow. My shoulder-length hair looks slightly curly. Seen in retrospect, I'm surprised by my wide smile. Although, upon closer inspection, I sense some tension. There is a forced rigidity that wants to scream out my wealth of aptitudes for carrying out the responsibility I've been charged with. But perhaps the most unsettling thing is that a lock of hair is almost completely covering one of my eyes, as if trying to keep the camera from capturing me entirely.

The position of my mouth and teeth, the angle of my eyes' openings, the direction of my gaze, the furrows on my brow. Any of it could be used against me. Physiognomy is a science that was once used to reveal our hidden character through our physical features. A prominent jaw, a wideness between the eyes, thick brows, or bulging pupils might have, for example, indicated my unequivocally demented nature to Renaissance physiognomists. My appearance could also be analysed to determine my capabilities as a mother. Throughout history, many people have encouraged husbands to examine the physical attributes of their future progenitors in search of defects.

The emergence of puerperal insanity coincided with the development of photographic methods. As such, we have hundreds of photos of Victorian madwomen. The camera was as crucial to the study of this type of madness, and later to hysteria, as the microscope was to histology. From the early nineteenth century, illustrations and photographs were used to exemplify mental illness and evaluate the progress of the institutionalised. One of these photos has stayed with me for a long time. It was in its caption that I first read the term 'puerperal insanity'. I am obsessed with this woman. Because she has three hands.

Her name is Emma Riches. She is wearing what in English asylums was called 'strong clothing', which wasn't exactly a straitjacket, but a sort of thick canvas dress that hampered movement and decreased the likelihood that patients would harm themselves.

None of Emma's words were recorded. I've been able to reconstruct fragments of her life from medical paperwork and admittance and release registries. Her insanity, like most throughout history, is a story told by others. The photo of Emma conveys an unsettling calmness, and I believe it is due to her faint smile, so mysterious that it makes her the Mona Lisa of the madwomen. On her lap we see a hand, the other seems half hidden on her right side, and a third hand grips the first. Whose hand is that?

In 1857, Emma was admitted to Bedlam asylum just months after giving birth to her second baby. Her first daughter had died shortly after birth. When she arrived at the hospital her family members explained that she didn't want to be with her son and that she had neglected her usual responsibilities. During the first few hours after her admittance, Emma was 'Constantly walking to and fro in her room, desponding and lamenting that she has committed some heinous offense for which she will never obtain pardon.' The doctors attributed her insanity to a strong hereditary predisposition, since her mother was locked up in another asylum and her aunt and maternal grandmother had died insane.

I try to imagine Emma discovering her first daughter dead. Did she walk over to the crib and find the baby was no longer breathing? Was she able to look at her lifeless body again? Was she now seeing her deceased firstborn in the face of the new baby? I visualise Emma wandering inside a dim room illuminated only by a sputtering gas light. A long skirt covers her petticoats. The guilt of the earth's first mother weighs on her and they've told her that her shoulders are too fragile to bear it. She walks in circles. Is it possible she feels panic that the nightmare will repeat when she approaches the newborn's crib? According to the doctors' notes, the response is a firm no. For them, everything lies in the madness she inherited.

There is a second photograph of Emma, almost a year after her admittance. We see her on the day of her release. She looks like a distinguished Victorian lady, holding a book. They would provide the madwomen with various accessories so the appearance of their portraits would fit with the ideals of female decorum. The artificiality of it all is even more evident when we read in Emma's medical history that she didn't even know how to read. But this photo is cause for optimism. Emma returned home, cured, to her son. And she lived happily. In the realm of sanity.

Or that's what I wanted to be true. The archivists of the former Bedlam asylum helped me to reconstruct Emma's life. I shared my obsession with them, and combing the records we learned that the story didn't have the happy ending I was hoping for. Emma had three more children and, every time, the same pattern repeated. She would give birth and a few weeks later she suffered a nervous breakdown. She was admitted to the asylum and, after nine or ten months, she would return home. Her behaviour became an accursed loop: her file reads that she would sometimes be in a state of 'feverish excitement, obscenity of language, delirium, & a desire to destroy furniture and linen' and other times that she 'stares vacantly, and takes no notice of anyone, not even her children, for whom she has previously shown the greatest affection & anxiety'. The unsettling alteration that characterised her first admittance shifted into a lethargic silence that never left her. The last entries in her medical records are the antithesis of hope.

'No changes'.

'Same state'.

'No improvement'.

'Same'.

Between her first admittance, at twenty-five years old, and her death, at forty-nine, she only spent seven years outside the asylum.

I keep asking myself who the third hand belongs to. The rational reader will say it belongs to a nurse, who was trying to keep her from hitting herself or touching the camera. I prefer to think that it's the hand of another madwoman, of her mother, her auntie, her grandmother, the madwomen of history. I see Emma's hand beside mine on my lap, when I am in my parliamentary seat, when they take my photo, on the train that brings me back home, and our two hands together are memory.

I retrace my path on that winged train. It is almost night by the time I reach the hospital and I cannot get in. Like a thing possessed, I robotically circle the perimeter of the maternity building.

I've been walking in circles for some time when night falls suddenly. The sun turns black and a red moon rises in a murky sky. I know that the hospital walls are about to crumble, that the bluish mountains on the horizon are collapsing. There is no one around me and everything seems ruinous. I have to enter. But the path to the door is covered in dross.

When I can no longer say how long I've been avoiding crossing that threshold, I search in my bag for my phone and I call my older sister. I cry with abandon. Finally I recover my fugitive voice and I confess to her that I don't have the strength to face seeing my children. That my fear is as great as my love for them. Horrified, I realise that phrase, which seems to emerge from hell itself, is coming out of my mouth. I can't breathe. I wish I could spit my whole self out, so I would have nothing to do with what I've just said. But it is too late.

My sister is my strength. And no one would have ever guessed that. Because she herself has broken down so many times that our family has lost count.

When she was a teenager, she spent almost an entire year without leaving the house. She was diagnosed with social phobia. I remember that my father, separated from my mother since we were very young, would come over and pull her by the arm to try to get her to go to school. He would only manage to drag her to the landing. My sister slipped away and ran back to lock herself in her cell. Her skin turned yellowish from the lack of sun. One day, my mother convinced her to go as far as the wide avenue behind the house, to sit on a bench so she could take photographs of her. When we got them developed, she appeared smiling, with that parchment skin. She seemed filled with desires. And I think she has made many of them come true.

Although it was a few years later than was typical, she went to university and got a degree. She is a young mother of two boys. She has a job she finds interesting. In psychiatric terms, she is a functional person. Freud defined mental health as the ability to love and to work. And my sister works a lot, but most of all she loves.

I call her and recite the anthology of ills that can befall my children, the symptoms I've been observing. She tries to reassure me, show me her support, offer me solutions. I begin to calm down. When we say goodbye, she says something that startles me: 'My niece and nephew are fine, there's nothing wrong with them.' What throws me off is that she calls them 'niece and nephew'. Because David and Sara are not just my children. They are her niece and nephew. They are grandchildren. They are siblings. It's not all on me alone. And then I start crying again. Because I just realised my vanity.

Humiliated, aware of my baseness, but feeling accompanied by my sister, I enter the hospital. I look upon my children and feel immense guilt. But I roll up my sleeves, change their nappies, and clean their skin of glass. I bring my face up close to theirs and pull it away while I recite sweet words with ridiculous diminutive endings. I kiss them and threaten to gobble up their toes that are grains of rice. I lose myself in the rituals of maternal love and for a moment I forget about the hooded figure with a scythe who, snubbed, watches the scene from the fluorescent ceiling fixture.

The next morning, when I awake, I have a message from my sister. It is a song by Franco Battiato, the guy who hit his nose against a pole as a boy and made his accident iconic.

'Ti proteggerò dalle paure delle ipocondrie,' he sings.

It has been said, and I like to think it's true, that this ode to love that is 'La cura' was dedicated to his mother, who died two years before it was recorded. Grazia Battiato was the pillar that supported that nose, and accompanied him on every tour and performance. She was the Sicilian mother who would elbow her way into the kitchens of the luxury hotels where they slept on tour and prepare a chamomile tea for her son's bellyache. The one who always trusted in his ability to create prodigious melodies. Towards the end of his life, when she had already left his side forever, the singer bought a castle in the Sicilian town of Milo and installed himself there to await death. And he had them reconstruct the chapel and had a priest give Mass in honour of his mother every morning.

> Ti solleverò dai dolori e dai tuoi sbalzi d'umore,
> dalle ossessioni delle tue manie.
> Ti salverò da ogni malinconia
> perché sei un essere speciale
> ed io avrò cura di te.

Death was a constant in Battiato's life. His little brother died at just four years old and, before the singer came of age, his father suffered a fatal stroke. Perhaps that was why he made his life and his songs a puzzle that erased the borders between the two worlds. Now, Franco Battiato rests in an urn beside his mother in the Riposto cemetery. But does death truly separate them? Battiato, like my sister, seems to have solutions for everything, even for neutralising the arrow of time.

> Supererò le correnti gravitazionali,
> lo spazio e la luce per non farti invecchiare.

For a while, as I remain lying in bed, with the Italian synthesisers in the background, I pretend that I too can overcome the gravitational pulls and I sway in my sister's childhood braids, with my mother and my dead father in the background.

Some days after the first parliamentary session, I post a brief text on social media. Two sentences in which I bemoan the fact that the spokespersons of every parliamentary group are men, even in the legislature with the most women ever. I declare that we still have work to do to reach equality and I manifest my feminist commitment to doing that work. Soon, my mother proudly lets me know that my words, and the photograph they'd taken of me in Parliament a few days earlier, are on the digital front page of the most important newspaper in the country. The urgency with which news stories unfold soon erases my celebrity, but that night I receive a call from another MP. He explains that he got a call from an assessor to our parliamentary group, who had in turn got one from an important man in the party. 'They are upset,' he tells me, 'and they asked me to tell you to be careful with what you post online, it can be manipulated by the press and end up looking like you are criticising our decisions, like what just happened.' I tell him that there was no manipulation, that the news item reproduced my words exactly, and that there was no malicious criticism, merely the statement of a shared weak point and the need to join forces to improve it. And I end the conversation.

That call reminds me of a game we used to play as kids. It was called Broken Telephone. Sitting in a circle in the schoolyard, we would whisper something in the ear of the child next to us. They would repeat what they thought they heard to the next one in the circle, also in a whisper, and so on and so on until the whisper had gone around the entire circle. We didn't know if the original message and the final one would have any resemblance to each other. And we revealed them amid giggles. I can't understand why we were still playing that game at our age, or why the angry man didn't call me directly. Nor did I understand why I had to silence the principles that in theory were the motivation behind my being included on the ballot. In that game of broken telephone, I realise, handcuffs have begun to grow around my wrists, tying me to the circle: I've taken on a debt with those who put me on the ballot, because they believed in me, but they owe me nothing for my having accepted, for the hours of work and for the sacrifices, for my having put body and mind into this project. I haven't even earned the right to be spoken to directly. The debts only move in one direction, and they are decided over phone calls that take place many kilometres away from me.

The room I'm in as I think all these things becomes an old place, with a dense smell of incense and someone speaks to me in a not-so-dead language: 'Turpe est enim mulieri loqui in ecclesia'. Saint Paul said that to the Corinthians: Let women be silent in the assemblies, they are not allowed to speak. His words come to me, today, twenty-one centuries later, as some sort of a conclusion to this game of broken telephone that, perhaps, wasn't so broken.

The writer Montserrat Roig recalled that, when she was in the university student union in the seventies, 'the young delegates only looked for "liberated women" at certain moments and after certain hours of the day'. It's likely that she was also invited to play the game of broken telephone, I think.

4

John Clare, with his long golden curls and bags under his eyes, was one of the most important working-class poets in England. In the eighteenth century he wrote combative odes to nature that denounced its destruction by man. But one day, Clare was robbed of language: 'Why, they have cut off my head and picked out all the letters in the alphabet – all the vowels and all the consonants and brought them out through my ears – and then they want me to write poetry. I can't do it.' He spent several decades in the asylums of High Beech and Northampton trying to get those letters back.

Experts say that anxiety is harder to recognise and diagnose than depression, because most of us find it almost impossible to express in words. That must have something to do with the fact that it's an alarm mechanism, a hyperbolic activation of the circuits of fear that turns us into trembling statues incapable of articulating any intelligible sound. They have cut off my head, too, and like the wolf's belly, they've filled it with heavy stones through which words cannot fly. That is why I've become obsessed with others' words. I've read lunatics from every era, men and women, living and dead. I have file cabinets filled with yellowed notes that are testament to the wonders I've found. This is, surely, the most important legacy I will leave my children. But it isn't easy to find these testimonies.

The history of insanity is too often the history of psychiatry. Samuel Tuke, the promotor of Victorian moral treatment, the same man who defended freeing the mad from iron chains, advocated for linguistic bondage. 'No advantage has been found to arise from reasoning with them, on their particular hallucinations ... In regard to melancholics, conversation on the subject of their despondency is found to be highly injudicious.' The insane were preferably silent and only a very few, mainly those who heard the calming clink of metal in their pockets, were able to break that silence.

Such was the case of Virginia Woolf, who bequeathed us some of the most lucid descriptions of anxiety. This 'rat gnaw' she called it. 'A painful wave swelling about the heart', the mind closing in on itself like 'a chrysalis'; that riding on a flat tyre. And in the face of that, she proposed more curious remedies, capable of discrediting the entire library of Alexandria of self-help: she refound joy 'uprooting thick dandelions & groundsel' or calmed herself by taking 'a census of happy people & unhappy'; she also managed to defeat depression thanks to an 'imperious need' to re-do the kitchen. But her primary therapy, which she recommended over and over again in her diary and applied to herself insistently, was mental activity, reading, and most of all writing. But for that, to be a writer, Woolf had to first become a murderer.

She confessed it in the paper she read at the National Society for Women's Service, in 1931. Every time she picked up her pen, she explained, a phantom came between her and the page, and tormented her ceaselessly. That spectre was a charming, altruistic, and above all pure woman. She answered to the name 'Angel in the house', that same angel who reigned in every Victorian home. And she would whisper to her: 'Be sympathetic; be tender; flatter; deceive; use all the arts and wiles of your sex' and never have your own preoccupations or desires. Virginia Woolf had to kill her – in self-defence, she argued. But it wasn't an easy task, and the writer had to fling her ink pot at her numerous times before she managed to be rid of her.

Now, so many years later, I also feel tempted to kill. The huge mass I was when pregnant has shrunk to nothing. The doctors express concern because I hardly eat, and I am a listless thing that could slip through the ventilation slats and disappear forever. The psychiatrist asks me to step on a scale and, when I do, I stare agape at the reading. How many kilos does my anxiety weigh, how many this phantom that dwells within me. I know that if I don't annihilate it, it and everything it has spawned, I won't be able to recover my voice. I try to identify the spectre that orders me to be pure, I try to hear the flutter of its petticoats, the flapping of its wings, to smell that unique aroma I've imbued it with. But I'm afraid that if I listen to Virginia and throw my ink pot at it, if I manage to annihilate it, there'll be nothing left of me.

During the weeks my children are in hospital, the psychiatrist suggests I turn this rat gnaw on my nape into words, and I attend several psychotherapy sessions with her. She wants to give me tools so I can kill my own phantoms, stain my hands with ink. Although I'm already sleeping back at home, I spend my days in the newborn ward, with David and Sara, and I only leave their side to go to the psychiatrist's office, which is in another building in the hospital complex, uphill, known as the 'former nursing school'. In the Victorian era, part of the moral treatment included the architecture and surroundings of the asylums. It was believed that beauty was fundamental to bringing the lost mind back to sanity. So, in the same period when Emma Riches was first admitted to Bedlam, a new superintendent, Dr William Charles Hood, attempted to transform the infamous institution into a bucolic place. He had the dusty floors covered with rugs, and the cold walls with robust libraries and art. He had green grass and flowers planted on the grounds. It seems nothing remains of all those ideas in the grey paved paths I now walk upon, flanked by weeds and hawthorn.

Despite the austerity and harshness of the space where the doctor receives me, I feel some peace with her. Her words have no hint of judgment, and in her gaze I can read that she doesn't consider me a bad mother. I struggle to talk about myself, and I often bring up political realities that concern me and she responds with frank answers. Dr Munt is an authority on perinatal mental health. We converse about the weight of poverty and the origin of so many mothers labelled as crazy; she confesses the enormous classist, racist, and sexist bias she fights every day to keep these women from losing custody of their children and entering into a spiral of institutional violence it's hard to escape. We often comment on the importance of the human factor in psychiatry, of which she is a palpable testament.

At the height of Victorian puerperal insanity, faced with the authoritarianism of many doctors, the obstetrician Robert Gooch stood out for his kind treatment of patients. That earned him the praise of his contemporaries, who were surprised at his ability to develop such close bonds with those common lunatics. Gooch was not immune to the sexism of his day, and he harshly criticised his patients for reading books, but he was able to see the link between mania and melancholy in women facing the severe test of new motherhood, and added significant doses of comprehension to the typical treatments. It's possible that his personal experience had something to do with this atypical empathy. Gooch was a melancholic man, who always lived closely with death and illness. His wife and daughter died within months of each other, and he himself suffered from a young age with the consequences of tuberculosis, which finally left him chained to the bed and snatched his life from him at only forty-five.

But Gooch's example did not spread, and many years had to pass before madwomen were listened to, understood, sympathised with. And it wasn't their pain that led the change. The mad began to be widely listened to, in twentieth-century England, and to verbalise their feelings and experiences, but not because of those Victorian cases of puerperal insanity, or even the plagues of female nervous disorders that invaded fin-de-siècle Europe. It was only when men began to be affected by an unprecedented syndrome that listening became widespread in psychiatry and trauma was recognised beyond Freudian sexuality.

During the Great War, hundreds of thousands of soldiers started trembling uncontrollably. Their hearts were racing erratically. Their bodies were twisting. They staggered when they walked. They cried and screamed. They didn't remember anything. Suddenly they turned blind and mute and were paralysed with no apparent injuries. But these soldiers couldn't be victims of insanity; some of them were true heroes, high-ranking officers. How could they be eccentric and degenerate lunatics? At first, these symptoms were attributed to invisible wounds to the nervous system caused by explosions – small indetectable haemorrhages. But that fallacy didn't hold up for very long, and it soon became evident that the wound was madness.

Kriegsneurose, shell shock, *obusite*. The war neurosis was finally defined, and Freud's ideas about the unconscious and the transformation of mental problems into physical symptoms were confirmed. The Great War was the apocalypse of masculinity. Many soldiers found themselves in a position similar to that of women of the period: completely impotent and without autonomy. The war, that savage and virile adventure, was meant to turn them into heroes but ended up confining them to a space as narrow as that of ordinary Victorian women, to the insanity that has historically assailed domestic captives.

Did those armies of madmen from the trenches and madwomen from the homes share a physical defect? Hippocrates explains that, when he learned that the Thracian philosopher Democritus was living far from society in a terrible demented state, he went to visit him to offer his wise help. He found him disembowelling dead animals and obsessively analysing their viscera to find the substance responsible for his melancholy. It seems that, despite his persistent efforts, he never did find it. But his fixation with locating the physical origin of his illness has continued to captivate science to this day. And the brain was and is the focus of all gazes.

On the other hand, Zeno of Citium, the founder of stoicism, declared that reason is not found in the brain but in the trachea, since that is where words emerge, and they are the sign of our rationality. Irrationality, then, could only be conjured by raising one's voice. And although I resist it, Dr Munt thinks that this is the only possible path for me. So, when my children have been released and we undertake the arduous road back home as a family, she assigns me to my local mental health centre, where they submit me to psychological as well as pharmacological therapy.

Before we say goodbye, the doctor jots down some final notes in my medical record: 'She persists with obsessive ideation around the health of her children and herself with constant verifications. There is a certain awareness of reality, but it is not clear if it is critical or not. She is ending her link to the hospital and I've assigned her to the Mental Health Centre.' And even though she leaves that unresolved question, her last words are a plea: 'Come see me again after some time has passed, with your children. I'd love to see you.' Because I am a mother, and I will continue to be. A normal mother, the kind who makes such courtesy visits. One day I will comb their hair, splash them with baby cologne, dress them elegantly, and tie hats on under their chins to protect their ears from the cold, and come see the doctor. And I will explain to her how adorable they are, that they've already taken their first steps or spoken their first words. These are my treasures, I will tell her.

When we bring the kids home I'm excessively nervous, as if I were about to receive the most important diplomats and world peace depended on me. I've tidied up everything, I've wiped every nook and cranny to eliminate even the slightest wisp of dust. I've watered the plants on the terrace so there is a brilliant greenness. I've lined up the glasses in the cabinet and polished the metal. When we arrive, Tomàs picks up the baby girl while I get the boy out of the carrycot and sit down with him on the oxblood velvet sofa. I stare at him to make sure he exists, that from the wasteland of my womb this thing truly emerged, this thing that surprisingly breathes, moves his body and points his gaze without anyone's assistance. His autonomy seems prodigious.

His father and I unpack a suitcase filled with homework. On one chart we are supposed to write down all the bowel movements and daily temperatures, record every nursing session, every three hours. They still weigh little and it is essential we maintain that frequency. The medical team will visit us to make sure everything is going fine. We are under some sort of house arrest, and knowing that someone is keeping watch on my mothering gives me some peace of mind.

Sara is pure crying. She doesn't like the house. I put my nipple in her mouth, but she doesn't calm down. I look around and think that the blue of the curtains that I chose so carefully isn't appropriate, that the crunch of the parquet floor with each rocking step I take is disconcerting to her, that the leaden bags under my eyes frighten her, that the touch of my hands is too rough for such thin skin, that there is nothing adequate in me or in the objects of my life and that the earth is sinking beneath our feet. Her father takes her and after a little while manages to calm her. This is a pattern that repeats over the following days and turns me into a small figure, distant on the horizon, a dot in the galaxy.

The first nights I set an alarm for every three hours to breastfeed them. Since my milk is insufficient, we complement it with bottles that their father gives them. We come up with a strategy to trick Chronos and rob Morpheus. We take turns, and that way we can sleep more hours in a row. But on my feedings, in addition to nursing and bottles, I have to wait for more milk to come in so I can pump for the next feeding. All in all, it takes me so long that I basically use up all of my down time. Furthermore, the solitude of those moments intensifies my fears, and a simple nappy change becomes an unsurmountable heroic feat. The gods are punishing my boldness, and at each shift I go a bit more mad.

Gradually, the house is becoming a gloomy mansion. A horrible cold has overtaken every room and the heating inexplicably fails to warm them up. The plants have lost their brilliance and the terrace is now a desolate realm where only a red carnation survives the harsh climate. The buzzing of mosquitoes I keep finding in the middle of winter perforates my eardrum like a legion of demons. At night, the shadows on the walls are insects that climb to the ceiling. If the spirits were allowed to return to our world, I have no doubt they would choose my house in the wee hours of the morning; there is nothing more terror-filled than my hands as they rush to read my children's temperatures on the thermometer.

I can't help but think about disasters that haven't yet happened. It is that anticipation that's one of the most damning features of anxiety. An anxious person's thoughts never anticipate happiness, but its opposite. My psychiatrist says that is because we unconsciously allow in past bad experiences that distort reality.

But my fears don't come from the past. The crushing reality is that danger exists and I have to do the impossible to avoid it. No mother, anywhere in the world, has escaped a stab when watching the mercury climb inside the glass tube. Mothers in ancient Egypt would sing spells to protect their infants from fever.

> Spell for a knot,
> for a child, a little bird:
> Are you warm in your nest?
> Are you burning in the bush?
> Bring me a little gold ball.
> Forty beads, a carnelian seal
> with a crocodile and a hand.
> That will protect you.

To reinforce that defensive wall of words, they would decorate the cribs with ribbons adorned with figures of fantastical animals, some armed with knives to kill anyone who tries to harm their children: 'Cut off the head of the enemy when he enters the room', they would write.

I have to be a thousand knives, and this feeling of constant alarm doesn't give me a moment's rest. Not even in the brief periods when I manage to fall asleep can I stop keeping track of my children's heart and breathing rates. When my mother calls or shows up punctually each morning, all I can articulate, in a wisp of a voice, is, 'I'm so tired.'

Few people know that the first victim of a transorbital lobotomy was a tired mother. In January 1946, Ellen Ionesco, a housewife, went with her six-year-old daughter to the office of Dr Walter Freeman in Washington, D.C. According to the little girl, her mother was so depressed she hadn't got out of bed in days. After exchanging a few words with Ellen, Dr Freeman, who sat in front of a wall covered with academic degrees, wrote in her file: 'She has suicidal ideas. She became more and more noisy, shouting: "I'm so tired, I'm so tired". I decided she was quite inaccessible and would require immediate treatment.'

The doctor led Ellen into a soundproof room and closed the heavy door. There he administered three electroconvulsive shocks, leaving Ellen unconscious. Then he introduced an instrument similar to an ice pick below her eyelid and hit it with a hammer to tap through her orbital cortex and penetrate her frontal lobes. With a quick movement, he severed part of her brain tissue. He repeated the operation in her other eye. When Ellen recovered consciousness after a few minutes, he gave her dark glasses to cover up the black eyes and told her she could return home.

The transorbital lobotomy was the assembly-line version of the first lobotomies realised by Portuguese Nobel laureate Egas Moniz. It was invented by Freeman, a young doctor who arrived at Saint Elizabeths mental hospital, in Washington, D.C., in 1924. Psychiatric institutions had unhealthy conditions and the patients regularly suffered mistreatment. Freeman was trained as a neurologist and firmly believed that the cause of mental illness was a physical defect in the brain. Obsessed with finding these defects, he would spend hours in the lab dissecting the brains of corpses to detect differences between the sane and the insane.

He was the doctor who brought Moniz's lobotomy to the United States in the 1930s and extended its use. According to Freeman, the operations were successful and managed to rescue a large number of patients from a life of chronic illness in psychiatric hospital wards. But it was too laborious, and World War II had left too many crazy people in its wake. To accelerate the process and allow the operation to drastically reduce the nearly half a million patients piling up in U.S. psychiatric hospitals, Freeman came up with a simple version that could be taught to anyone in just twenty minutes. That was how the transorbital lobotomy was born.

Freeman became a spectacular showman, travelling around the whole country demonstrating his prodigious invention, and eliciting the admiration of all his psychiatric colleagues. On one memorable occasion, in West Virginia, he lobotomised thirty-five women in one afternoon. Although the cases that have made history are those of people from well-to-do society, such as Rosemary Kennedy, the sister of the president, most patients were marginalised crazy folk banished by society. At the Lakin State Hospital for the Colored Insane, for example, Freeman practiced more than a hundred and fifty lobotomies on poor black patients whose names we will never know.

In the mid-1950s, the first studies on the long-term consequences of the lobotomy were published: many people were left in a vegetative state, and those who weren't had serious difficulties carrying on a normal life. The medical elite repudiated lobotomies with the same fervour with which they'd embrace them as miraculous.

But Freeman was unwilling to renounce his revolutionary invention and the glory it had brought him. He moved to California and started practicing lobotomies on another type of patient, children with behavioural problems. He lobotomised nineteen minors, one of whom was four years old. By 1967, he had performed more than 2,900 lobotomies. In February of that year he did his last one, which ended with the patient dying from a brain haemorrhage.

In the last years of his life, Freeman obsessively drove around the country looking for his patients to prove that lobotomies were not the disaster that was then claimed. The dispenser of reason was searching for comfort in the mad.

I wonder if he spoke with Ellen Ionesco and if she told him that she was still tired. Some years ago, before my children were born, I found a volume titled *La folle histoire des idées folles en psychiatrie* in a French bookstore. It is a sort of decalogue of the crazy things psychiatry has done in the name of reason and, of course, the lobotomy made the list. But the fact that they are no longer performed doesn't mean that psychiatry has completely renounced overstepping its rightful bounds in attempts to control patients. The words of psychiatrist R. D. Laing point an accusatory finger at millions of psychiatric offices around the world: 'In the best places, where straitjackets are abolished, doors are unlocked, leucotomies largely forgone, these can be replaced by more subtle lobotomies and tranquillizers that place the bars of Bedlam and the locked doors *inside* the patient.'

On my first visit, the psychiatrist at the health centre confirms the diagnosis of anxiety associated with postpartum and validates the pharmacological treatment. He suggests that for a while I forget about my professional responsibilities, but I refuse to. Parliament doesn't have maternity or paternity leave like other jobs do. The only possible option is telematic voting but that would mean giving up taking part in the debates, the meetings, cutting off communication with the civil society that has put its trust in me. We've just assaulted the skies, and regular women like me have managed to slip through the clouds and make a place for ourselves. I can't leave my seat empty. Luckily, since the government hasn't been formed yet, parliamentary activity is not very intense and I have a little break. I hope to have recovered by the time I need to participate fully.

The first medically documented case of postpartum depression in history was described by the Portuguese doctor João Rodrigues de Castelo Branco in 1551. The patient was 'the lovely wife of Carcinator', who was attacked by melancholy after giving birth and remained mad for a month. A month, a month of pain and panic, is acceptable, I think, and I would be willing to sign off on that, to sell my soul in exchange for that. But not every case has such a rapid recovery. Dr Strecker, already in the twentieth century, tells of a postpartum psychosis that is cured only after seventeen years: 'For ten years she was confused and stuporose, unresponsive and filthy in her habits. Thereafter she showed alternating periods of violence and depression. In the thirteenth year she began to converse, with a tendency to mimicry. She gradually became clear and alert, neat and tidy, and developed remarkable skills in embroidery and fancy sewing.' It's possible that this poor raving woman's child saw his mother sane for the first time at his graduation ceremony or eighteenth birthday, and wondered who that calm woman looking at him proudly was.

Throughout history, all sorts of treatments have tried to accelerate the healing processes, from poppy syrup, bloodletting, and morphine to electroconvulsive shock therapy, those blue volts that sizzled the poet Sylvia Plath 'like a desert prophet'. Today the indisputable queen is pharmacological therapy, which presides over my bedside table in a plastic bottle, promising salvation. Every period has tried to decipher the causes of postpartum madness, but even today, in the era of DNA and quantum mechanics, they remain in the dark. In Victorian England it was attributed to either a milk metastasis, an irritation of the breasts or uterus, or to alterations of the vascular system brought on by childbirth. Various obstetricians argued that the use of forceps to accelerate birth could prevent women from going mad, while others were of the opposite opinion. A baby's large head could also be the cause, since it was believed that the madness began just in the moment that it came through the cervix. Today hormones are considered the prime biological culprit. In my case there is also a previous history of anxiety, an infertility treatment, and an arsenal of family precedents that would make any psychoanalyst's mouth water.

I try to convince the psychiatrist that no, that isn't what's wrong with me, that it is all much more simple and much more terrible, that, as the poet John Donne said, 'we have a winding sheet in our mother's womb, which grows with us from our conception', and that I have seen this shroud, I keep seeing it every time I look at Sara and David. I wove it myself,

I tell him, during those months they were in my womb, and I was unable to give them the gift of immortality.

What mother wouldn't make her children invincible, what mother wouldn't give everything for them to never die. The nymph Thetis knew that her son Achilles was mortal, and she wanted to protect him with all her cunning. So, when he was born she bathed him in the black waters of the River Styx, which granted immortality. But when she dipped him in, Thetis held the baby by his heel and that part of his body, untouched by the magic waters, became his point of vulnerability. All his mother's efforts were in vain, even dressing him as a little girl and raising him among women so he would not be sent into battle. In the Trojan War, his enemy Paris shot an arrow into his heel, killing him. While I ponder what my children's Achilles' heel will be, the psychiatrist looks at me with pity and schedules a session for the following week.

5

My children's bodies grow while mine dwindles and returns to its prior state, before pregnancy. The afterpains, a unique word in the maternal dictionary, are due precisely to that process. The apricot that is the uterus measures seven centimetres and weighs seventy grams. But during gestation it becomes gigantic and multiplies in size by ten. The afterpains are cramps that come without warning and shake up that massive apricot, while you are changing a nappy, giving a bottle, or pumping your breasts; they are the excruciating reminders that your body is getting used to its regular emptiness and tedium.

I had never confronted my body the way I did during pregnancy. I had never appreciated it. My body had always been a site of mocking and illness. As a girl, my long thin fingers elicited among my classmates all sorts of comparisons to aliens, and excessive sweating made me loathe my hands and try to constantly keep them behind my back. Then there was a dermatological affliction that left me with a bald patch on my head, giving me – at only six years old – the appearance of a small lost Franciscan monk. I got used to wearing a hat, summer and winter, to cover, more than just that patch, all my other shameful bits.

During my pregnancy, I not only had to expose my naked body to medical staff, but the machines insisted on revealing my innards. The constant ultrasound scans put me in contact with a part of me I had struggled to ignore. And all of them featured a muscular surface covered in shadows, the uterus, the source, according to Hippocrates, of six hundred maladies, including madness. For the Greeks, the uterus was like a person possessed by the desire for children. If it remained barren for a long time, they said, it would grow irritated and enraged. Then, explained Plato, it would wander 'in every direction through the body, close up the passages of the breath, and, by obstructing respiration, drive them to extremity, causing all varieties of disease'. In antiquity, the wandering womb particularly affected virgins and widows, or childless women. They would lose their voice, choke, gnaw their teeth, roll their eyes back in their heads. It was the Greek word for uterus, *hystéra*, that lent its name to the woman's madness par excellence.

An amulet from the fourth century BC says 'Womb, I say to you, stay in your place', and in the Museo Nazionalle Etrusco di Villa Giulia, in Rome, tourists admire ex-votos that represent wombs in the form of small fish, with little wings and rounded silhouettes. Because the uterus was a naughty animal inside another animal, which wandered capriciously from side to side and up and down throughout the whole body, gnawing on the organs it encountered along the way. Since it was attracted to good smells but repelled by disgusting ones, scent was how to get it back in place. If it was in the upper part of the body, blocking the throat of a patient who had suddenly gone mute, the doctor would burn smelly substances beneath her nose. According to my gynaecologist, the wings of my womb had nothing to do with the fact that every aroma made me nauseous at the start of my pregnancy. The guilty party, she explained to me, was called chorionic gonadotropin, a hormone that apparently looks nothing like a fish.

During my entire pregnancy, I would feel very unsettled by that dark, cavernous image appearing on the monitor as I lay on the examination table. I would look at it out of the corner of my eye, and only focussed on it when it was pointed directly at either Foetus A or Foetus B. Then, squinting, I made a superhuman effort to fix my eyes on them, to keep my gaze from flying away from their tiny bodies and onto some centimetre of my own. 'The body has been made so problematic for women that it has often seemed easier to shrug it off and travel as a disembodied spirit', wrote Adrienne Rich in 1976, and her words seem to still have the power of timelessness. In Renaissance Italy, the first thing a woman did when she discovered she was with child was write her will. In the nineteenth century, many doctors attributed puerperal insanity to the fear of dying in childbirth. The experience of Princess Charlotte, the daughter of King George IV, whose wealth could not save her from dying in childbirth at just twenty-one, marked an era. On the day you read this, according to the World Health Organisation, more than eight hundred women will die trying to become mothers. But the hooded figure with the scythe knows something about classes and is particularly vicious with mothers who live in the poorest countries. Not even the American dream is safe: in the United States, women of colour have much higher probabilities of dying in childbirth.

Pregnancy forced me to confront my body; motherhood insists I accept that we are flesh and blood. Because I am the one who probes my children's kidneys and hearts, the one who trims their nails and wipes their bottoms. The word 'mother' comes from the Latin *mater*, also the root of matter, of everything that has a physical existence. But not even that etymological bluntness is capable of encompassing the exhaustiveness of the experience. We mothers spend a good chunk of our time devoted to details of the bodies of our babies. We discover the tonalities of their skin, the anomalies, scars, blotches. We accept that there is no such thing as a uniform body. There is a corporeal omnipresence that forces me to accept that, as much as I try to deny it, both the babies and I live in and through our bodies. And I soon learn that those bodies are the asset I want to protect more than anything: their tiny wrists, the clefts in their clavicles, their miniature bright red earlobes.

In the early 1970s, the poet Sharon Olds sent her work to a magazine for their consideration. She was taken aback by the response:

> This is a literary magazine. If you wish to write about this sort of subject, may we suggest the Ladies' Home Journal. The true subjects of poetry are ... male subjects, not your children.

Sharon Olds made her children's bodies – slender, viscous, gleaming – the centre of many of her poems. Through them parade the quotidian tasks of a mother; fear of fever, a broken bone, a coughing fit; the paediatric medications that fill the shelves or the particular expression each of her children makes while sleeping. But the man running the magazine found the poems to be banal, concerned with female subjects, not fit for great art. I would've liked to speak with him and explain that one day my father and I saw death. And then, with all the valour of which man is capable, instead of fleeing, I remained there, at the foot of that hospital bed, and I fed him, I wiped his ass, and I read him stories over the last days of his life. Just as Roland Barthes did by the bed of his moribund mother. In his 19 November 1978 diary entry, he explains exactly what had happened to him: '[Status confusion]. For months, I have been her mother. It is as if I had lost my daughter (a greater grief than that? It had never occurred to me).' Sharon Olds, Roland Barthes and I want to reveal a secret to that editor, whisper it in his ear: the experience of caregiving awakens a desire to protect that is nearly limitless, and that is what truly illuminates the greatest themes of all time, because injustices are not abstract, but concrete wounds that batter living, breathing bodies.

At Cape Canaveral, on Tuesday 28 January 1986 at 1600 hours, 39 minutes, and 13 seconds, seven of those bodies exploded in the sky. To the horror of millions of spectators, the Challenger space shuttle became a ball of fire shortly after taking off with five men and two women on board. One of them was the teacher Christa McAuliffe, the first civilian to travel to space. She was chosen as part of a campaign to increase the popularity and prestige of the space race. Years earlier, NASA's new project, which allowed for ships to be reused, sought to once again put the United States at the top of the space race. In order to do so, Congress approved an enormous budget allocation. But the gleam of what was known as the 'space shuttle era' soon faded. Technical problems kept them from completing their ambitious launch schedule. The political class was upset about the spending, and, in the eyes of the public, the number of missions was turning the adventure of the stars into something routine.

NASA needed to do something spectacular, and it decided to send the first ever non-professional crew member into space. That way every American would feel like a potential astronaut. They spent weeks considering a thousand names. Many were in favour of the chosen civilian being a poet, an experienced troubadour who could sing to the stars. But President Ronald Reagan had something else in mind, and he announced it in a press room filled with journalists: 'When the shuttle lifts off, all of America will be reminded of the crucial role teachers and education play in the life of our nation.' And, among eleven thousand candidates, Christa was chosen. A normal young woman, relatable, like us, a wife and mother of two. Sharon Olds dedicated a poem to her and her death, 'For and Against Knowledge'. The poet imagines Christa McAuliffe at the moment of the explosion, but transmuted into her own daughter:

> If she were my daughter,
> I'd want to know how she died – was she
> torn apart, was she burned

The poet put herself in the place of Christa's parents, who were at Cape Canaveral with five hundred other spectators watching the launch. Parents who enthusiastically shouted out the countdown along with their daughter's students, who from an auditorium of the high school blew noisemakers moments before it all ended. Seventy-three seconds after launching, there was a blinding explosion. Christa's mother and father don't understand what is happening. Is that fire normal? When the ball of flames plunges into the ocean, like Olds in her poem, they only want to know one thing: where is their daughter? The metaphysics don't matter, Olds wants the body.

> And the spirit –
> I have never understood the spirit,
> all I know is the shape it takes,
> this wavering flame of flesh. Those
> who know about the spirit may tell you
> where she is, and why.

Soon the NASA engineers informed Christa's parents that a major malfunction had occurred, which in their language means that several disasters converged and there are no survivors. The next day, with America in mourning, Reagan tried to console his fellow citizens with another poet's words, and declared that the seven astronauts, now national heroes, had slipped the surly bonds of earth to touch the face of God. But that is not what Olds wants:

> What I want
> to do is find each cell,
> slip it out of the fishes' mouths,
> ash in the tree, soot in your eyes
> where she enters our lives, I want to play it
> backwards, burning jigsaw puzzle
> of flesh suck in its million stars
> to meet, in the sky, boiling metal
> fly back
> together, and cool.
> Pull that rocket
> back down
> surely to earth, open the hatch
> and draw them out like fresh puppies,
> sort them out, family by family, go
> away, disperse, do not meet here.

Over the next months, thanks to an expert investigative commission, it was discovered that the shuttle had had previous technical problems and that numerous engineers had warned of the possibility of a catastrophe. On the day of the disaster, icicles sixty centimetres long covered part of the spacecraft and they foresaw that low temperatures could deteriorate the Challenger's weak point, its O-ring seals. Some of the mechanics communicated this to the heads of NASA, in an isolated control room, but their words fell on deaf ears. It turns out this was the source of the explosion, a ruined piece of rubber and negligence on the part of the NASA directors. William R. Lucas, supervising the liftoff, decided to proceed despite the warnings. 'Going into space is something that great countries do. It's also risky; you have to take some chances,' he said years later in an interview, from a comfortable armchair in his detached Tennessee home.

The term continues and we still don't have a new president to lead the government. But the plenary sessions and commissions begin to function normally, and I have to combine childrearing with trips to the capital. Before leaving, always in the early morning, I count the clouds and make impossible calculations about the raindrops threatening my children's cribs. I give detailed instructions to their father, who will remain on call. Whenever anyone asks, I say I'm proud of this inversion of roles, but deep down it's torturous. The aridness of the desert I cross as the sun rises reminds me that more than a million paces will separate me from David and Sara over the coming hours. Madrid represents the crying of children that are not mine. I can walk carefree, even happily having lunch with colleagues in restaurants, but when a baby cries at the next table seven swords pierce my heart.

I see David and Sara in every legislative proposal, in every verdict. Many mothers have joined forces throughout history to demand social justice. I've never thought that motherhood automatically makes you a better person, nor that there are feelings only felt by biological mothers. If I ever feel tempted towards that naive essentialism, I am flooded with images of Aryan women with chubby babies in their arms encouraging their compatriots to commit the worst atrocities in the name of their descendants. I find refuge from the contradictions that accompany me in this political and maternal adventure in the work of Sara Ruddick. She coined the term 'maternal thinking' to refer to the feelings and commitments those of us who rear children acquire, which often lead us to share and defend an ethical position that listens to the pain of others. This wasn't about biology as had so often been asserted:

there is no one on earth who can't learn maternal thinking. It is through the recognition of this thinking that we can take back motherhood from the narrow private framing of the patriarchy and detonate it in politics.

'We are hungry, we have no coal, we have no clothing or shoes to wear. Our children are cold and have no food. How can we go on this way? Today we were a few women in the Drassanes shantytown, tomorrow it will be the entire district; then, all the women of Barcelona, and if that's not enough and our demands aren't heard, we propose closing the factories and we will resort to asking for solidarity not only from the women of Barcelona, but from all the elements that make up societies and cannot live in these current circumstances,' shouted Amàlia Alegre, a militant of the Radical Party, to an enthusiastic crowd in January 1918. Days earlier, near my home, she and thousands of women started a revolt to protest the brutal rise in the cost of coal and basic products. They attacked trucks and occupied a warehouse on Carrer del Parlament to the yell of 'Out with the speculators! Women to the streets to defend ourselves against hunger!' According to a journalist of the period, the officers in charge of keeping order, were beleaguered by the shouting women: 'If the authorities don't manage to contain the rising prices, our housewives will take care of it, just as they've been managing heroic feats with our domestic economies for some time.'

With the passing years, the memory of Amàlia Alegre and so many other women has faded among the male allegories of the revolutionary labour force. But I felt compelled by David and Sara to keep it alive. My children are the embodiment of the reasons for remembering this history. In one plenary session that is burned into my memory, I touch their bodies kilometres away and share the anger of eighty-one fathers and mothers who have lost their children.

On 24 July 2013, a train accident happened in Angrois, an area in Santiago de Compostela. Today the victims are in the stands of the chamber to attend the debate about creating the investigative commission they've been demanding for some time. The Angrois derailment is a case that brings together the worst of a bipartisan system, which sealed a pact of silence about the truth behind dozens of deaths. Because, as revealed in the horrific documentary on the incident, *Frankenstein 04155*, in the systematic alternating of the government between the two parties, they both shared responsibilities for an accident that could have been avoided. And in that session, it was also clear that the interests of construction companies too often trump the safety of the bodies of our families we take such care to protect.

I'm moved listening to the words of the victims quoted in the addresses by some of the politicians. 'Ladies and gentlemen, do not cause us any more pain.' That is the burden of our responsibility that day, and it is so meagre. We aren't in time to avoid the real sting, all we can settle for is not rubbing more salt in their wounds. And we are not even capable of that. At the end of the session, the bipartisanism is united in its lack of compassion. The no votes exasperate the victims present. Shouts of 'truth', 'justice', 'no more lies' are heard. The president asks for the public to be escorted out and, while the chamber guards invite them to leave, a few of us get to our feet and applaud their fruitless bravery.

Reviewing the session records as I write this, I see that the stenographer documented the exclamation of one female member of congress: 'Shameful'. I have no idea if I was the one who said that, and for a moment I hope I was. But that narcissistic wish merely proves my impotence that day.

NASA wanted the world to look on with admiration while it conquered the most distant star in the universe. Our leaders wanted a train that connected the capital with the periphery at the speed of light. But Amàlia Alegre and her contemporaries just wanted coal so their children wouldn't freeze to death. Mothers are powerful. We mould the brave, as Napoleon said. But how impotent that mould becomes in the face of powers that mercilessly lay waste to every seed we sow.

My nervous breakdowns are constant and intense, and the psychiatrist decides to transfer me to the Anxiety Unit at the Hospital del Mar. Accustomed to the darkness filling my normal days, the first morning I visit there is a burst of light. The hospital overlooks one of the beaches of the Barceloneta, and I hadn't seen the sea since I became a mother. Unlike the typical Mediterranean calm, that morning it is strangely choppy, as if a serpent were tossing it and awakening its waves. I order it to settle down, but it remains as disobedient as my head.

Jaume, the psychologist who sees me, immediately focuses on my hypochondria. Outside, the sea batters the rusty railings on the breakwater with the same force as I am battered by the certainty that I'm suffering from hundreds of illnesses. Many women with puerperal insanity were convinced, as I am, that death was waiting for them right outside the doctor's office. In 1852, in the winding halls of the Edinburgh asylum, Jean Main begged her doctors to give her medications to tame the balls of fire burning her throat and to operate on her rotting intestines. According to her medical records, she was sure she had 'all the maladies the flesh is heir to'. There was no consoling Jean; when they refused to do what she asked, she threatened the staff with violence and swore she would crack their skulls. There is no consoling me either, as I remain lethargically silent across the desk as Jaume takes notes. There was also no comforting that American hypochondriac who, I once read, had his tombstone engraved with 'I told you I was sick'.

The history of hypochondria is as old as humanity; from the first spark of the Big Bang someone has believed they could see their death foretold in every flash of a distant star. The term was first used by Hippocrates in the fourth century BC, from *hupo*, 'under', and *khondros*, 'sternal cartilage', to describe various problems of the spleen, liver, and gallbladder. Over time, it took on its current meaning, since that was the area of the body where hypochondriacs said they were feeling the pain that would kill them. The Renaissance doctor André du Laurens described three types of melancholy: one that comes solely from the brain; one that sympathetically proceeds from the whole body; and one that is produced in hypochondria, mine, which links me to those who have the most poetic symptoms in the history of madness. Books of ancient medicine tell us of the cases of anonymous hypochondriacs who are, nonetheless, the most famous in history. Like that man who believed his feet were made of glass and refused to walk so he wouldn't break them. Or the baker convinced he was made of butter and couldn't be persuaded to go anywhere near the oven, sure he would melt. One man was so frightened by seeing a crocodile that he became certain that he had lost an arm and a leg and acted as if he didn't have them. He escaped the danger the crocodile presented, but he could not escape himself. My favourite is the case of the Greek poet Peisander of Camirus, who thought that his soul had fled his body and lived scared to death that he would run into it somewhere.

I explain to Jaume that, if that happened to me, if I came across my soul and could show it to him, it would be such a dark shade of black that it would burden his senses. And it would give off the most repulsive aromas. The scent of guilt and death. The scent of children's disappointment at having learned, even before they could speak, how weak their mother is. I tell him that there is no purity in the mother who sits before him, that I live in the filthy squalor of incompetence and writhing deformity. 'Ah, purity,' he answers, smiling. Then he speaks of my ordinariness, of how this purity I so desire doesn't really exist. 'There is nothing filthier than the human mind,' he says. He explains that among the most common symptoms of postpartum anxiety are precisely these intrusive, repetitive, and persistent thoughts about the horror that paralyses me and that, in extreme cases, these thoughts lead new mothers to a phobic avoidance of their babies. 'We have to work to keep you from reaching that extreme,' he declares as he immortalises in his computer everything I'm ashamed of.

I leave the hospital. The sea continues to be a boiling pot, but I no longer care. What is killing me is that burst of light, clarity. I run to the stop and board the bus, emptied of energy. I long for the curtains of my bedroom like a thirst. The Ancient Greeks believed that the cause of melancholy was an excess of one of the four humours, black bile. The darkness of that liquid, according to Galen, caused the melancholic's brain to turn murky, and – just as the night is scary, not only to children, but also to the bravest among us – melancholics live in an eternal night that makes them permanently afraid. Our souls have grown used to the perpetual fog and we are enemies of the sun. I arrive home sobbing and only calm down when I draw the curtains. My children sleep in their cradles. I barely glance at them. Is this all I can offer them, a rampant evasion of every heavenly body?

6

The days pass and surprisingly everything seems to be going fine. My children are like two machines that function perfectly. I am amazed to think that I was the one who created these Swiss watch mechanisms, which gain weight at a constant rhythm and meet the paediatrician's expectations. Even though I don't ever completely relax, there are moments when I manage sparks of unawareness in what I intuit would be a peaceful life with them: snuggles and laughter on a backdrop that is no longer so gloomy, sometimes even gleaming with the precious metals of all the treasures that could harbour there. Tomàs and I, on the days when I'm in Barcelona, get into the habit of walking up a nearby hill. The streets that head there are steep and, to avoid the pram from slipping out of our hands, we put a lead on it and around Tomàs's wrist. And like that, firm and heads held high, we stroll with those two little gems beneath a thousand wool blankets. When we reach the highest point of the little bluish mountain, after crossing civilised terraced gardens and conquering the pine forest at the peak, the misty city opens up at our feet. In the distance, the sea is so immense that I wonder if the kids can even perceive it. When I was a little girl, my mother would explain that ants couldn't see me, they are so tiny, she would say, that their brain can't process the existence of something so gigantic. You, my children, are not even an atom of this immense ocean and yet my entire existence depends on you.

One morning, Sara wakes up with a cough. She'd been coughing a little bit the day before, but the doctor didn't think it was anything to worry about and told us that we should only bring her in if the coughing continued. This morning, she is coughing more. She barely weighs two kilos.

Her father brings her back to the health centre. I stay with David and tell Tomàs to ask the doctor if we can go out for a walk when they get back. While she coughs, I think about walking up the hill with them again. That was what was in my mind, going for a walk. When you relax, when you free yourself from the shackles of your fear, that's when devastation strikes.

The children's author Maurice Sendak explained in an interview that when his father would come home happy, pleased about some good news, his mother would quiet him with a loud, sinister 'Sssssssh': 'Don't tease God into striking you dead by walking around saying . . . you feel fine,' she would say. I wanted to go out for a walk and the universe won't forgive me for it. Shortly after Tomàs leaves the house, he calls me. They are about to admit Sara to the Sant Joan de Déu children's hospital. She has bronchiolitis.

My daughter has mucus, too much mucus, and her tiny bronchial tubes can't expel it. A few days later they confirm that the bronchiolitis has provoked RSV, respiratory syncytial virus. In an adult it's like a simple cold, but in some babies, especially if they're premature, it can be quite serious. During the time we spend in hospital, I learn that, in the winter months, the fearsome RSV is an epidemic that fills the paediatric emergency rooms with children gasping for breath.

We spend a few days in the room, with an oxygen mask and cortisone to keep the inflammation under control. I imagine myself walking up the bluish mountain again with Sara, but I know that the pine trees have lost their needles. I'm convinced that the seas we glimpsed just days ago are drying up. Every few hours, the doctors interrupt my apocalyptic reflections and come into the room to listen to Sara's breathing with a stethoscope. That instrument, so essential for keeping tabs on my daughter's condition, seems, compared to the shining monitors and digital thermometers, like an artifact from another century. Through it they listen to her sibilant rhonchus. And even though the term sounds somewhat magical, it hides a much more sinister reality. At first it seems that Sara's lungs are small but strong, and the nurses say she will recover. But there is a concert in her alveoli that sounds increasingly like a funeral march.

One Sunday she's taken a turn for the worse and they have to increase her amount of oxygen several times. At dusk I am nursing her and, even though she wants to latch onto my nipple, even though she's starving, I can tell she is grasping for breath. I want to nourish my daughter, and a tyrant is stealing her air. The parade of doctors and nurses begins, and for a moment I think that even I can hear her sibilant rhonchus. At midnight I hear it clearly, shouting in my ear. And I tell the doctors, she's suffocating, and the world with her.

Finally, they decide to transfer her to the ICU. There they put a mask on her that could belong to a scuba diver or a Hollywood psychopath. Behind it I think I can sense her crying, but I can't manage to hear anything. My daughter is suspended in time. She has hands and can't touch; she has feet and can't walk; her throat emits no sound. I ask the doctors what will happen to her. They say we have to wait and see how she progresses. And I just want to rip pages off the calendar.

I pick up her tiny hand, finding it covered with many tubes and cables. I look at our two hands together. At the entrance to the paediatric floor there is a large sign that reads 'Careful hand washing kills RSV'. After seeing this, no matter how often I wash them, no matter how hard I scrub, I feel like my hands are dirty. I want to go back in time and wash them, to before the virus, before infecting Sara with the corruption of my skin. In the days that follow they will start to crack, I'll even have injuries from the harshness of my scrubbing them against terrycloth and paper towels, but I won't manage to turn back time.

Sara moves, she's restless, she complains. Little by little she relaxes until she falls asleep. There can only be one companion in the ICU, and I am close to collapsing. In the early morning, Tomàs relieves me and I go home to rest with David. Before I leave, the doctor warns me: if she doesn't respond, we'll have to take further measures.

When I get home I watch how, in his crib, David dreams obliviously. My mother is snoring beside him. I sit on the sofa, my eyes wide open. I just want to rest a little bit, keeping my phone nearby, with my mind in the ICU, beside Sara, on call. But I fall asleep, as if I have no shame. It has begun to rain and the drops beat on the glass panes. I incorporate the drumming rain into my dream. The terrace is filled with frogs that bang on the windows to get into the living room, I know they want to jump on top of me, on top of Sara, on top of everything that's alive, and I cannot allow that. I push the door to keep them from busting it down, but their strength sends me to the floor. Suddenly, I'm awoken by a phone call. They've intubated my daughter. While I was lying down, defeated by the dream and the frogs.

The ICU is like a space control centre. At its core are the computers that engineers and mechanics use to supervise the machines, which are the bodies of our children; the ships where the infants are cured are scattered around a universe that is the room, with a thousand monitors that every so often send out a warning. The hours of waiting are long, tedious. For a moment, you can forget where you are. Until an alarm goes off, and you look up at your child's monitor and selfishly plead for it not to be theirs that's sounding.

Sometimes the alarms go off for banal reasons. A cord got disconnected or a sensor isn't working the way it should. In Sara's case, the alarm usually signalled a drop in oxygen. Then the nurses would rush over to her body and, with an instrument whose name I don't know, manually inflate her with air. This operation reminded me of when a fireplace flame is about to die and you use a bellows to revive it. That is sort of what they were trying to do with my daughter, to keep her flame from going out.

In a number of languages, the word for bellows is related to the word 'crazy'. *Fool* in English, *fou* in French, and *foll* in Catalan come from the Latin word *follis*, which was the term for that leather bag filled with air. We have heads filled with air. The same air that keeps the fire burning, the same air that gives life. That's all we mortals are, a breath.

It is always night in the ICU. Without any natural light, not even my shift changes with Tomàs remind me that day exists. On each bed there is a place to put the patient's name, which is normally decorated with cartoonish drawings so that we don't forget we are in a children's space. When I show up one day to relieve Tomàs, I see that next to Sara's name he has placed a drawing he made.

The sketch shows a newborn Sara, with almost imperceptible peach fuzz and veins filtering through the thin skin on her head, but she stands completely upright. Dressed in the Elizabethan style, with a ruff around her neck and a solemn sash, she holds a sword.

This Shakespearian Sara makes me think of Cordelia, her mad father, and one of the saddest scenes in the history of literature. As his daughter lies dead in his arms, towards the end of the play, King Lear implores:

Why should a dog, a horse, a rat, have life,
And thou no breath at all?

But my little Cordelia has a sword. And she is breathing; through a machine, but breathing. Before Cordelia dies, when she still has a wisp of life, Lear makes her a promise:

> So we'll live,
> And pray, and sing, and tell old tales, and laugh
> At gilded butterflies, and hear poor rogues
> Talk of court news; and we'll talk with them too –
> Who loses and who wins; who's in, who's out –
> And take upon 's the mystery of things,
> As if we were God's spies; and we'll wear out,
> In a wall'd prison, packs and sects of great ones
> That ebb and flow by th' moon.

They couldn't do it, Sara; we will.

One of the things that most surprises my family is my supposed composure throughout this situation. But nothing could be further from the truth. I have an immense support network for me and my children that allows me to keep up a sane appearance while my madness spreads.

During the months after giving birth, I suffer from telogen effluvium, which is the weakening and massive loss of hair. I've always had the bad habit of running my hand through my tresses and these days I often get a handful of hair. But one afternoon, when I'm alone, I feel the desire to rip out chunks, and I do, without thinking twice. I compulsively stuff the hair into my mouth, to my surprise. I remember when I was a little girl, on a visit to the zoo, I saw the famous albino gorilla Snowflake do exactly the same thing. In front of a rowdy crowd of spectators, he would tear out his fur with no shame, leaving a trail of blotches of pink skin. Then he swallowed it. Without batting an eyelash. As if it were the most normal thing in the world.

Gradually, I was mutating into an animal and my reason was deserting me. Beasts and madness have always been linked. The Bible warns us that if you ignore His voice, 'the Lord shall smite thee with madness, and blindness, and astonishment of heart', and that is exactly what He does to Nebuchadnezzar, the arrogant Babylonian King whom He punishes. Nebuchadnezzar's greatness had grown so much that it reached the heavens, and his sovereignty spread to the ends of the earth. Despite the divine warnings he received in a dream, the King continued with his opulent expansion. The Almighty then decided that he would drive him from people and he would live like an animal: 'Let him be drenched with the dew of heaven, and let him live with the animals among the plants of the earth. Let his mind be changed from that of a man and let him be given the mind of an animal.' Thus he lived for seven years, until he was forgiven. William Blake immortalised him on all fours in a cave, with hair like eagle feathers, curved claws, and a gaze lost in madness.

One day, while I'm pumping the milk that will later be fed to Sara through a tube, I'm afraid that the hair I'm devouring will contaminate my daughter's sustenance. When I get to the hospital, with the little bottle in a portable cooler, I remain at the threshold, ask for a doctor to come over, and confess everything. That when no one is looking I rip out my hair and eat it, like Snowflake, I tell him, and I don't want them to give my daughter this poisoned milk. The doctor looks at me incredulously and says there's no problem, the milk is fine, and that I should talk to a psychiatrist about it. He takes the little bottle and leaves. His surprise and coldness embarrass me and are a blast of reality. I'm a crazy mum and I shouldn't have said anything. Those words reverberate in my head as I write this, but for some reason I'm incapable of deleting them.

When I speak with the psychologist he tells me that what's happening to me is a phenomenon that occurs with high levels of anxiety. It's called trichophagia. In extreme cases, the hair ends up forming balls in the stomach that have to be surgically extracted. Later I read that it is common in animals in captivity, especially simians, who use this method to try to placate their imprisoned restlessness.

In *The Divine Comedy*, Dante exemplifies madness as a punishment for a crazy mum turned into an animal. Her name is Hecuba, Queen of Troy, famous for her fertility and, according to Euripides, she gave birth to fifty children. After the fall of Troy, Hecuba has lost her kingdom and almost all her children. Imprisoned by the Greek enemy, her only comfort is having her daughter Polyxena by her side and knowing that her son Polydorus survives with all his wealth, protected by the King of Thrace. But her captors decide to sacrifice Polyxena, and while Hecuba is bemoaning her death by the sea, she glimpses among the waves the body of her son, the only child she thought was still alive. 'I cannot, cannot credit this fresh sight I see,' she cries. Upon discovering he'd been killed by his supposed saviour, the Thracian king, for his fortune, Hecuba plots a terrible vengeance: with the help of other Trojan prisoners, many of them venerable mothers, she blinds the murderer and stabs his sons. 'Thou wilt become a dog with bloodshot eyes,' the wounded king curses her. The people of Thrace, enraged by her atrocious crimes, attack Hecuba with stones; but, with a harsh growl, she chases them and tries to bite them; when she opens her mouth to speak, she barks. Turned into a dog, she is condemned to suffer as a beast for all eternity.

Dante and Virgil find Hecuba in the tenth and final pit of the eighth circle of hell. Beside Satan himself there are charlatans and forgers and plagiarists; their punishment is leprosy, oedema, and madness. And there lies Queen Hecuba, tormented by the vision of her dead children.

Out of her senses, [she] barked as would a dog;
so greatly had her suffering turned her mind.

It hasn't stopped raining since the frogs invaded my terrace. For the last ten days the heavens have remained open and downpours obliterate everything. Tomàs and I alternate shifts at the ICU, and on the way from the hospital to the taxi stand, the rain drenches my clothes.

One day, a nurse comments how lucky I am to have such a father for my children. 'Usually they don't spend as much time here as the mothers do,' she confesses. I sense a reproach in her words and I leave with my head bowed.

Suddenly, one morning, when I arrive at the ICU, I feel the breeze between my skin and the dry clothes. And that is when I figure it out. The waves are rough but harmless, they howl but don't bite. A rainbow of seven bright colours makes its way through the clouds and Sara opens her eyes.

By the tenth day Sara is considerably improved and they take out the breathing tube. They have me leave the ICU and, when I come back in, I find her waking up, gradually, as if from a nap, as if she were just stretching. She seems to be repeating the words of her first paediatrician, 'life finds a way', with hardly a care in the world.

We stay in the hospital for a few more days until she is released. The doctors tell us that it's very likely Sara will have delicate lungs. She'll get bronchitis repeatedly and maybe even asthma. And they are right. Both she and David, in the first years of their lives, will have one respiratory crisis after another.

The psychoanalyst Franz Alexander coined the term 'asthmatogenic mother'. In the 1930s, he was the first to discuss psychosomatic disorders, which included a large number of ailments. But these all pointed to the same culprit, the mother. Asthma, as Alexander details in his influential treatise *Psychosomatic Medicine* (1950), conceals a repressed dependence on one's mother. The asthmatogenic mother is one who displays an 'open rejection' and the spasming bronchial tubes of her child are his desire towards her: an asthma attack is 'a cry for the mother'. Was Sara crying for me, behind the immense mass of cords, during her induced sleep? I force myself to think about their small premature lungs every time David or Sara have a crisis. I invoke my scientific and feminist side, draw on the litany of critiques of psychoanalysis that I've read throughout my life, but Alexander's accusatory finger points at me from his respectable tomb.

The ultimate asthmatogenic mother is Jeanne Clémence Weil Proust. Biographers and critics have unanimously blamed her for the poor health of the celebrated writer. From birth Marcel Proust is a fragile, sickly child, who will soon display an exaggeratedly sensitive temperament, with explosions of rage and tears in the face of any setback. At nine years old he suffers his first asthma attack on his way back from a walk with his family. He has such trouble breathing that they fear for his life. His father, a doctor, does not know how to cure him. Finally, he sits him down and makes sure he remains positioned very straight by leaning him up against his voluminous medical manuals. Only then does his attack subside.

Proust's love for his mother was extreme and, according to the Proust scholars, he maintained an excessively intimate relationship with her throughout his life. The nun who cares for her on her deathbed would later say to the writer: 'To her, you were still four years old.' And after her passing, he lamented that 'my life has lost its only objective, its only sweetness, its only love, its only comfort'.

Alice Miller, the renowned psychologist and psychoanalyst who produced extensive and celebrated work on child abuse, declares categorically that the asthma Proust suffered his whole life and his death of pneumonia were due to a mother who was too present and controlling. He breathed in too much air ('love') and he wasn't allowed to breathe it out again ('control').

The first few months after his mother's death, Proust is incapable of reacting, and his inactivity is, perhaps, the consequence of too much passion. For him, there is no love without *angoisse*. But gradually that love makes him react. In a letter, he confesses to his friend Maurice Duplay:

> When I lost my mother, I wanted to disappear. Not to kill myself, because I didn't want to end up in the

newspapers, but rather slip away from lack of food and sleep. I then thought that with me would disappear the memory I retained of her, that memory of a unique fervour, and that I would drag her to a second death, this one definitive; that I would be committing some sort of parricide.

The idea of parricide towards his mother would haunt him for the rest of his life. The great biographers have focussed on the pain Madame Proust provoked in her son, and not much on the reverse, the suffering Marcel Proust inflicted on his mother, despite that idea obsessing him. 'She loved me a hundred times too much since I now have the double torment of thinking she could have known, and how anxiously known, that she was leaving me, and above all of thinking that the whole of the end of her life was so afflicted, so constantly preoccupied with my health.' He constantly blames himself for having been too demanding and hard on her, and for having caused her, with his bad habits, a lethal anguish.

Almost two years after the death of Madame Proust, her writer son reads in the newspaper that an old acquaintance from French high society, Henri van Blarenberghe, has stabbed his mother to death, although he loved her madly. Proust is profoundly impacted by the poor victim's last words; when she realised it was her own son who had stabbed the knife into her, she dragged herself to the stairway and, shortly before falling there, raised her arms and said, 'What have you done to me, Henri, what have you done to me'. A month later, Proust publishes in *Le Figaro* a text titled 'Filial Sentiments of a Parricide', in which he reflects on the murder and ends up identifying with the killer and confessing that he too killed his mother, and that, in a way, we all do:

'What have you done to me! What have you done to me!' If we think of it, there may not be a single truly loving mother who would not be able, on her final day and often long before, to reproach her son with these words. Deep down, we kill all those who love us, we age them with the anxiety we cause them, with that kind of uneasy tenderness we inspire in them, that constant state of alarm.

I live obsessed with my children's health, with the pain my insanity might cause them, but I don't ever think about my mother, who, most likely, from some corner of the world, is shouting along with Proust's mother: 'What have you done to me!'

When we return home from hospital with Sara, my mother is waiting there for us. She is happy. She looks at me, contented, and I respond with a reproachful glance. 'Ssssssh!' Like Mrs Sendak, I fear the wrath of heaven. The first trial is over but there could be more to come. It's been some time since I let my mother be happy over anything, and she has gradually adopted the identity of a tortoise.

During the fertility treatment, when my ovaries confirmed their barrenness, every morning I would be subjected to an ultrasound so they could count and measure my oocytes. And it was basically a wasteland. When I left, I would transmit the verdict to my sister and to Tomàs, and I kept that ovarian desolation quiet from the rest of the world. My sister would communicate it to my mother, who every afternoon, as her only message, sent me an emoji of a tortoise. It was her way of telling me that little by little, everything would turn out fine.

But I also think that she was telling me that she was a tortoise. Willing to stick her head into her shell if she was bothersome, and, if I needed her, to come out and find me silently and without getting in the way. An ancient, eternal tortoise, without the right to disappear, because I was constantly telling her that she had to take care of herself, that I still needed her. I always saw her as some sort of multi-use device in perpetual motion, that could be forced to speak to me or become silent, or from whom I could demand consolation for all the evils of the world or demand that she ignore my pain, someone I could just as easily accuse of drowning me with too much attention as reproach for her negligence.

My mother explained to everyone who would listen an old legend that authors like Jacint Verdaguer and Joaquín Dicenta turned into poetry in the nineteenth century. A kind young man who is attentive to his mother falls in love with an evil woman. She asks him, as proof of his love, to serve her his mother's heart on a tray. The young man, blinded by desire, shows up in his mother's room and, as she sleeps, rips out her heart. Fleeing with his trophy in his arms, he falls to the ground and with him falls his mother's heart, which lets out her last words:

Just as he reaches the doorway of
His star most bright,
He stumbles—the heart now asks her son,
"Are you all right?"

According to my mother and that poem, written in the splendour of the idealisation of the angel in the house, a mother's heart never forgets that its main ache is for her child.

I've always blamed my mother for being the living example of that ideology of sacrifice, but I've also taken advantage of this and perpetuated it. The poet Lynn Sukenick named this phenomenon 'matrophobia': we reject our mothers, are panicked at the thought of turning into the self-sacrificing and martyrised women they are, because it is easier to blame the individual than to recognise and combat the forces acting upon her.

Mothers are doomed to failure. Because there are falls in every life. And since we are the point of entrance into life in this world, there is nothing easier than blaming us. There is a spotlight that blinds us and submits us to the greatest of scrutinies, we bear the curse of motherhood under vigilance:

we are mocked when our displays of affection and concern are excessive; we are criminalised when judged to have neglected our children. In patriarchy's kitchen, women can never find the right quantities of the ingredients that make up good motherhood. No woman is ever glorified for being a mother to her kids, after all, it is part of her instinct; but if she doesn't do it, she becomes the embodiment of evil.

Mothers live in the realm of powerless responsibility, according to Adrienne Rich. Babies are extremely dependent on their mothers, but little by little they learn that this maternal power is accompanied by an excessive impotence. Oh, how that formidable maternal presence shrinks when the storm worsens and she must face a judge, a social worker, or a real estate executive.

They also watched my mother through the peephole as she raised us. Divorced when we were little, she was accused of spoiling us and, at the same time, not spending enough money on us. At her place of work, which she shared with my father and his new wife, there was the rumour that she spent the child support with her new boyfriend and dressed us in rags she bought at Sepu, a department store on the Ramblas famous for its poor quality and lack of aesthetic appeal.

I can hardly conceive of the humiliation my mother must have felt and, like I so often do, I delved into it. How they accused her, made demands on her, looked down on her, how they blamed her for our family's collapse and all the injustices of the world, including the ones she suffered. How I never allowed her the right to make a mistake, how much leeway I gave my father in comparison. Now that I'm a mother, sometimes it keeps me up at night, thinking about all that, about what I said to her that day, what I wrote to her the other day, and I call her; I wake her up in the wee hours without the slightest consideration and I tell her, mum, I can't sleep because of what I did, because I didn't realise, because of how I ruined that Epiphany celebration for you, your birthday party, the thousands of evenings when you came home from work defeated and I, like a leech, demanded more and more, and then less and less. And she tells me that doesn't matter, that she loves me, that she was happy with me and my sister, that she only remembers the good things. And I get angry, and I tell her to get upset remembering it, at least a little, please. We get into a loop that borders on comic. Then, in an extremely sweet voice, she asks me to get some rest, says that she's fine, and I hang up aware that, even if she weren't, she wouldn't tell me.

Over time I've learned to recognise that my mother, somehow, hit upon a clairvoyant joy. A joy that comprehends there are limits to a mother's job, that imperfection exists, that disaster could happen at any moment but you have to act as if it were impossible. My mother turned her lamentations into dancing to the rhythms of the ballad singers whose records she played on Sunday mornings. It wasn't that she was oblivious, not at all, but she decided that most of the time she would rather keep the hair shirt in the closet.

I, on the other hand, even now, when I finally have my daughter back in my arms, healthy, just out of hospital, can't stop with the flagellation. I look at my mother out of the corner of my eye. She's smiling at me and I hate her for not hating me, not even in that moment.

7

The history of evolution is narrated as the triumph of reason over emotion, as the farewell to our primitive animality, which only blooms occasionally to bear witness to how we've managed to dominate it. 'With mankind some expressions, such as the bristling of the hair under the influence of extreme terror, or the uncovering of the teeth under that of furious rage, can hardly be understood, except on the belief that man once existed in a much lower and animal-like condition,' wrote Charles Darwin. But Darwin himself often bristled, sweated excessively, and his heart raced as if he were facing a carnivorous predator. And that predator was the fear of illness.

The son of a doctor, Darwin began studying medicine, but he soon shifted to geology and natural sciences. One of the weighty reasons behind that decision, he would explain years later, was the profound impression that two operations that ended tragically made on him, one of them on a young boy. That sad sight would obsess him for years. In his autobiography, Darwin confessed how hypochondriacal panic overcame him as he was waiting to set sail on the *Beagle*:

> Those two months at Plymouth were the most miserable which I ever spent, I was out of spirits at the thought of leaving all my family and friends for so long a time. I was also troubled with palpitations and pain about the heart, and like so many a young ignorant man, was convinced that I had heart disease. I did not consult a doctor, as I fully expected to hear the verdict that I was not fit for the voyage, and I was resolved to go at all hazards.

That worry would plague him his entire life. He frequently vomited and suffered from constant stomach pain, exhaustion, tremors, dizziness, and nausea. He left a chronicle of all the aches and pains that vexed him in his health diary and in various notes for his physicians. On a typical day in 1835, for example, he wrote:

> For 25 years extreme spasmodic daily & nightly flatulence: occasional vomiting; on two occasions prolonged during months ..., hysterical crying dying sensations or half-faint. & copious very palid urine. Now vomiting & every paroxys[m] of flatulence preceded by singing of ears, rocking, treading on air & vision ... All fatigues, specially reading, brings on these Head symptoms ... nervousness when E. leaves me.

None of the twenty doctors he consulted could give him a precise diagnosis. Historians have scoured the thousands of handwritten pages of his letters and diaries in search of symptoms. Even though they offered various explanations, some as far-fetched as a strange allergy to the pigeons he used in his experiments, they haven't reached any definitive conclusion and the nervous origin of his illnesses continues to be the most plausible.

Darwin's poor health, which to him felt horribly real, led him to live a life of increasing reclusion. His nerves deteriorated with any social commitments, and visits from family and friends to his rural home made him profoundly agitated and disrupted his sleep. He would lie awake terrified at night, but with occasional sparks of lucidity that made everything even more ridiculous: 'my reason mocks me and tells me I need fear nothing.'

Since my children were born, I also spend hours in the dark, trembling. Every night is dashed with awakenings soaked in sweat that lead me to foresee disasters. I fear for my children's health but also for my own. My skin becomes a minefield, and seeing a splotch, freckle, or lump could blow up the world at any moment. I'm constantly palpating myself, going so far as to give myself bruises that later make me uneasy as if I didn't know where they came from. And I begin to shun looking at my own body. The surrounding darkness is gaining ground. I shower with the lights off, I comb my hair in the shadows, I dress in the gleam that enters from the hall. And I avoid mirrors. Like a lady in a horror film, afraid that the candle in her hand will illuminate the ghost behind her, I look away every time any surface reflects back my image.

I begin to submit my family to long interrogations over every symptom. It hurts here, what could it be? Can you feel this bulge in my inner thigh? Do you see this freckle I didn't have before? This dizziness isn't normal. The web woven by hypochondria takes control of everything around me. My persistence and insatiability end up confusing everyone, and there comes a time when no one is able to distinguish health from sickness. In this gloomy mansion I've turned our home into, we no longer walk on steady ground.

I undergo cognitive-behavioural therapy with Jaume, whose objective is to give me practical tools I can use immediately to help me modify my behaviour. Jaume assigns me small challenges that to me seem like epic feats: turning on the lights for some of my personal hygiene tasks; not constantly examining my body; and, like a modest lady, I am to very gradually reveal my pale extremities in front of the mirror. And, most of all, he wants me to quit the tangled mess of doctors' appointments I involve everyone around me in; he says they are more addictive to me than the most powerful opioid. To that end, he meets with my family and orders them to ignore my pleading. Since then, when I desperately call them over some unequivocal sign of serious illness, my family must repeat like a mantra that they love me and because of that refuse to feed my obsession.

In the evening, sitting on the sofa in silence, when the children are already sleeping, I feel that Tomàs is so distant from me that I can't even see him with binoculars. I blame him for his lack of understanding and I have no intention of trying to seek him out. I'm oblivious to the fact that he is also burning up in the hell I've created of my first few months of motherhood. I wander through our home offended but I also occasionally mumble out an apology for all my missteps. I'm victim and executioner, and I've left no role for him. I do, however, demand he have the perfect response at all times. In the face of every symptom, and every doubt. And he never gets it right.

Jaume and experience tell me that there is no consoling a hypochondriac. Any validation is fleeting, because the truth of the evidence soon dissolves and the voracious fear is shifted onto another, even worse symptom. Charles Darwin had his father, a doctor, to assist him throughout his life. But his responses never satisfied him. 'I told him about the insensitivity of my fingertips,' he wrote in a letter to his wife Emma, 'but his only reflection was "yes, yes, of course, it is a neuralgia, yes, yes, of course!"'

The history of humanity is also the history of a search for the cure for hypochondria. Before electroshock therapy and anti-psychotics were used as weapons of mass destruction on the hypochondriac imagination, ingenuity was a powerful medicine. This was detailed by Robert Burton, the English clergyman, who in 1621 published his compendium *The Anatomy of Melancholy*, in which he explains over hundreds of pages all the ills of insanity. When treating hypochondria, he suggests highly curious remedies. Like the woman convinced she'd swallowed a snake: her doctor gave her an emetic and placed a snake like the one she described into the bucket of vomit and, when she saw it, she was cured. Or the case of a gentleman from Siena who refused to urinate out of a fear of flooding the city. The doctor had the bells rung and told him there was a fire, then he peed and was instantly cured.

But there is nothing beautiful in hypochondria, because it is the greatest of paradoxes: its sufferers fear illness so much that they become ill with hypochondria; and they so fear death that they don't truly experience life. 'The fear of death is worse than death,' states Burton himself, who also suffered acute melancholy. In one chapter of the book, titled 'Digression of Air', he explains that this was precisely the reason why he wrote his long treatise: to find the cause and remedy for that vast ill that tormented him. Because while we believe we live in the era of anxiety, *The Anatomy of Melancholy* was a true bestseller in its time, with six reprintings, probably bought by the legions of melancholics who were seeking comfort in its pages.

It seems that Burton himself was able to find some consolation. The origin of his melancholy, he wrote, lay in his obsessive desire to know 'in what consists the existence and designs of God'. Without a cassock, from my intellectual vantage point as a convinced atheist, I bang my head against the same walls as Burton did in his stubborn attempt to control the world's chaos. After he died it was rumoured that

Burton, aware that this was impossible, had hanged himself in his own church. 'If there is hell on earth, it is found in the heart of a melancholy man,' he wrote. And it is very likely that, after his death, if he saw the face of the God to whom he had prayed so much, he was seated to His left.

The left is the territory of hypochondriacs. The side where, according to the Bible, the foolish of heart sit, is also the one melancholics lean towards. That's where it hurts, say those who suffer from imaginary ailments. Science offers an unromantic explanation: it could simply be a question of the layout of the viscera; for example, intestinal gases usually cause pain on the left side, since the spleen is an obstacle in their path.

The frontispiece of *The Anatomy of Melancholy* contains an illustration of various types of melancholics. *Hypochondriacus* is shown crestfallen in a leather tunic, leaning of course towards the left and with his head resting on his left hand while he looks distractedly at the bottles of medicines and apothecary formulas scattered on the floor. His poem makes his suffering clear:

> Wind in his side doth him much harm,
> And troubles him full sore, God knows

When we close the volume, after reading of the horrors of the hypochondriac, Burton offers us a final message. There is hope for the miserable, there are threats to the happy:

Sperate miseri; cavete felices.

Since Sara was released from hospital, the doctors have recommended we exercise extreme caution for some time to avoid her catching another virus. There is a part of the ICU that hasn't entirely left us. In the period before the pandemic, we were already wearing masks around the house and had hydroalcoholic gel in every room. And I still maintain the same state of alert, and I walk among imaginary monitors and cords.

One night when my mother-in-law is visiting, nearly a month after Sara comes home, as I am changing her nappy, I notice a slight crack in her sob: a subtle aphonia that makes me disproportionately upset. I cry and dishevel my hair; I am sweating, dizzy, trembling. I carry her into the living room. Tomàs and his mother confirm that, yes, her voice is hoarse, and that we should take her to the doctor the next morning. But I refuse to wait. This time I won't be caught off-guard. I'm convinced that only rapid action will save her from the ICU bellows, and I tell them that I'm taking her to the emergency room. Tomàs and my mother-in-law think it is a bad idea, that it's late, cold outside, and that the waiting room of the children's hospital will be filled with dangers for sensitive bronchioles. But I have made my decision. As I walk to the door, my mother-in-law gets up off the sofa and rips Sara from my arms: 'Don't take her. You are being selfish. You aren't thinking about her health, just about your own peace of mind.'

My laments stop suddenly. I've been transported without warning into a domestic Gothic novel where a poor mother is driven mad by a cold, cruel family, led by an evil mother-in-law. I tell her to give me my daughter and leave my house. She looks at her son. He asks her to do as I say, please.

I grab Sara and, through the window, see the sky disappearing like a parchment scroll rolling up.

We take a taxi to the emergency room. I've imposed my will on Tomàs, prevailed over his pleading for me to see reason, to wait for the morning, to temper my passions. I am holding Sara firmly in my arms. That's when Tomàs says it. 'What a mother these poor kids are stuck with.'

Like a point-blank bullet, those words conjure up a large chapter of history – that of the bad mothers – and their ghosts materialise and sit beside me, one after the other. The overprotective mothers, the domineering, the castrating, the possessive, the toxic, the narcissistic, the smothering, the manipulating, the absent, the distant. All of them, piled up, are with me in the back seat of this car drawn by snakes, crossing the city of Barcelona. 'My children! What a rotten mother you're stuck with!' shout millions of fathers to all these Medeas with eternal bags under their eyes.

Medea is the paradigm of the perverse mother who has tortured our collective imagination for centuries. The murder of children by the woman who bore them is the cruellest of acts, an abominable deed that unleashes terror over a mistreated mother's destructive power. Medea is the spiteful mother, the abandoned woman who takes revenge in the most scandalous way. The words Euripides has her say to her husband Jason at the end of the tragedy resonate everywhere: 'But the children are dead: this will wound you to the quick.'

I've sought justifications for Medea in each of the verses she speaks, in the chorus, in her cruel husband's replies, in every one of Euripides's stage directions. And the play is certainly filled with political reasons. 'Of all creatures that have breath and sensation, we women are the most unfortunate,' she reveals. In a deplorable exception to the usual rules, it is the woman who buys her master, with a dowry to her husband. And pity she who makes a mistake in her choice, because while the man can abandon his wife at any time, she is destined to live always subjugated to him. And while the great odes sing of male bravery, ay, she bemoaned, 'I would rather stand three times with a shield in battle than give birth once.'

After I become a mother, I obsessively reread *Medea* and in its words I discover a love for one's children and for material needs that I hadn't grasped before. Because of her husband's ambitious love for a new woman, Medea and her innocent offspring will be exiled, condemned to the misery of statelessness and homelessness. Medea, like so many dispossessed mothers throughout history, is on the other side of wealth and power, with her children as her only bulwark. She begs for them, breaks down, and manages to avoid her children's exile. But that does not give her the insatiable security that a mother seeks: 'By Hell's avenging furies, I shall never leave my children for my enemies to outrage.'

After a thousand hesitations, a thousand ambivalences, she takes the decision. The children are doomed, and now it is her womb which speaks: 'They must die in any case. And since they must, the one who gave them birth shall kill them.'

Twentieth-century feminism claimed Medea from the darkness she'd been painted with, and saw her as a revolutionary. The philosopher Slavoj Žižek deems the murder of her children to be an act of absolute liberation from patriarchal law. But with Sara in my arms, as I try to wrest her from the grips of illness, and with David sleeping placidly, oblivious to the world's suffering, I can't stop thinking about Medea's children, and how revolutionary their still being alive would be. Few people even remember the names of the murdered children, Mermerus and Pheres, and hardly anyone saw them die. In Euripides' play, the crime takes place offstage, and in the film adaptations it is also not depicted. But we hear their voices. And they are terribly human and real. Why hadn't I ever stopped to listen to them? They ask for help, they ask for compassion:

> Oh, what shall I do? How can I escape my mother's hands?
> I know not, dear brother. We are done for.

Finally, they break into a cry: 'We are now close to the snare of the sword.' There is a moment in the tragedy when the coryphaeus considers intervening to stop the murder.

> Shall I enter the house? I am determined to stop the death of the children.

One of the infants begs him:

> Yes, in heaven's name, stop it! Now is the time.

I extend my arms. I want to enter the printed page, extract those children, save them from maternal impotence, pain, blindness. But they are no longer breathing. And Medea, converted into a sorceress, flees with the cadavers in a flying chariot given to her by her grandfather, none other than the Sun-God. Because such an atrocious mother cannot be human. The last words that Jason addresses to the murderous mother echo throughout history:

> Children, what an evil mother you got.

There is a painting at the Prado, made by Germán Hernández Amores in the late nineteenth century, in which Medea flees with her dead children from Corinth through a tempestuous sky. What most impresses me is the weight conveyed by the lifeless bodies of Mermerus and Pheres, an unbearable, inexpressible weight that is somewhat born on the backs of all mothers. Because when we arrive at the hospital, with Tomàs's words still echoing in my ears, I think that Sara is staring at me, and I wonder if she can't also feel the snare of the sword.

The emergency room doctor reassures us. Sara has a sore throat, probably viral in origin. Back in the hospital, that leaden voice from when we lived in the ICU returns to me, and the questions keep coming. I won't leave until I'm certain it won't turn into something serious. And there is no way to get the response I'm looking for. It isn't likely, but the virus could move into her lungs. And if that happens, it's possible, although also not likely, that she might have to be transferred to the ICU. Over time, I've learned that everything could end up moving into my children's lungs: a slight gust of cold wind; the dripping of a gentle rain on their cheeks. A sneeze, a cough, a hoarseness, a little knee sticking out from under the blanket on a winter night, and the sirens go off. After I've cornered the paediatrician in a spiral of pleading, she reluctantly offers me something akin to a certainty: if she doesn't get worse in twenty-four hours, we can rule out anything serious. And those twenty-four hours pass – every minute, every second that is a century, a millennium – with my ear glued to Sara's chest, lying in wait for any sign of wheezing. And her voice gets clearer, and she inhales and exhales, and nothing hinders that routine magic. Trumpets sound, the sky returns to its rightful place, and once again the morning star shines.

That isn't always the case. During the twins' first few years, there are many visits to the emergency room in the wee hours and regular hospital stays. Approximately a year after that visit, the oxygen mask is insufficient and Sara ends up in the ICU. Creation howls and I again feel labour pains. By that point, the government had been established; the conservative party remained in power. I spent Tuesday through

Thursday in Madrid each week, when the plenary sessions and committee meetings were held. When re-entering the perpetual night of the ICU, I maintain a bit of lucidity and pounce on a nurse: I urgently need a document to justify my absence in Parliament, allowing me to vote remotely. Soon after, they hand me an official paper detailing my daughter's illness and its severity. I'm saved, I can hold Sara's hand, make sure her heart is beating, that she isn't gasping for air; I can keep the bellows at arm's length, fighting by her side with the sword of my eyes.

But that isn't what happens. A few hours after I send in that justification of my absence, I receive a call from the President of Parliament. She is a veteran MP who practiced medicine before becoming involved in politics. She says that she's very sorry, that she understands from her own experience the situation with my daughter, but that she can't let me vote virtually. The rules are strict and, according to the regulations, such voting can only be allowed in the case of maternity or paternity leave, or a serious health crisis affecting the MP themselves. Any other case is excluded. I speak with my parliamentary group and they are firm: I must go to Madrid. There is an important vote and the result will be decided by few ballots.

On the docket that week in Parliament is a decree proposed by the government that, with the pretext of updating the labour regulations for stevedores, is trying to liberalise those regulations while cutting dock workers' salaries and rights. It is vital to those affected that this measure does not pass, but also because it would establish an important precedent: another victory in a privatising strategy whose objective is fattening the coffers of the large multinationals. Furthermore, in order to garner the public support the measure lacks, the government and part of the media have presented the stevedores as rough but privileged men, dark Melvillian characters with salaries higher than average and a work stability that most of the population envies. They want to set the common people against each other, to make the stevedores gnaw on the same stale bread as the rest of the working class, instead of everyone aspiring to the bankers' fine fare.

Since neither the parliament nor my party are able to offer me an alternative, I leave the ICU early the next morning and head to the train station. During the three-hour trip, my tears cloud the landscape I already know by heart, where the meridian is marked by the beauty of that desert that today seems more lunar than ever. When I reach the chamber there is a euphoric atmosphere. We are going to defeat the government's decree, and it is the first time that's happened since 1979. But I have the feeling I am entering an ice kingdom. I see the walls crumbling, the staircase invaded by grass, the halls covered in weeds. Dust accumulates everywhere and all the gilding seems rusty. The stevedores are watching us from the gallery. Some of my colleagues are wearing T-shirts that say 'You dock my world'. The speeches are moving, the debate speaks of dignity, of the people, of freedom. And we win.

One of the MPs on the left bench announces during his speech that the government wanted to debate this decree today because three of the MPs who intended to vote against it are on an official trip to the United Nations headquarters in New York. But things have not gone as they'd planned. Those MPs have already landed and are on their way to Parliament. He says their names. One part of the chamber bursts into loud applause. I think about my daughter, in an

ICU more than six-hundred kilometres away, fighting every three seconds to get a bit of oxygen into her lungs.

I look at my hands, which are applauding the heroic journey of those three MPs, but aren't holding my daughter. And the only thing I want is to go back home.

The decree fails. In the end the vote wasn't as close as had been expected. One of the MPs in my parliamentary group even made a mistake when voting, but he is forgiven amid giggles. After all, to err is human. Some days later, my daughter also laughs, already released from the ICU, and I laugh with her. At some point during the term I will read a study which says that in developed countries, 9 per cent of male ministers are childless compared to 45 per cent of female ministers. I write that down in my agenda, so I won't forget it.

An entire architectural vocabulary has come up around the many difficulties women encounter when trying to participate in politics. During my years in Parliament, I learned it all: cement walls, the glass ceiling and walls, the sticky floor. I often contemplate the abyss of the glass precipice, into which so many women have fallen, pushed by competition and risk-taking while men watched from their secure positions. Even if they get back up and flee politics, the wounds from the fall will haunt them for the rest of their lives. But what surprises me most is the intricate glass labyrinth that awaits all women who enter politics, a path that is filled with obstacles and cul de sacs, with no arrows or maps, and, most of all, one that is immensely lonely. It seems that men with our same qualifications and experience have been handed the ball of thread and can navigate the labyrinth without much difficulty. They leave us to deal with the minotaur.

It was this way, that way; to the right and then veer left, there's no way out here; this looks familiar, we've been this way before; this is impossible, turn around, this is a dead end. Those are some of the things you hear in the labyrinth in the district of Horta, a few metro stops from my house. It was built in the early nineteenth century with cypress walls and arches in the middle of a lovely romantic garden. In the Middle Ages, they would build labyrinths in front of churches so that the devil, so mischievous, would be drawn in and get trapped and distracted, allowing the pastor to enter the church safely. When my kids are a bit older and can run steadily, we often walk through that labyrinth of trees, like three disorientated devils, amid laughter, shouting, tickles, and joyful exasperation. When we make our way out, we find a small greenish lake, and behind it, in a grotto hung with ferns, the beautiful nymph Echo congratulates us on our escape. Right beside her, a plaque reads:

> Both in love – that much is true
> when Death, surreptitious
> finds Echo and Narcissus;
> she loves him and he loves him, too.

Charles Darwin was obsessed with the idea that his children would inherit the physical illness he was convinced he suffered from, but he never thought about how the fear of illness could take root in his entire family. According to the guides I read in my desperation, it is easy to transmit the habit of hypochondria from parents to children, and that seems to be what happened in the Darwin family. Of the seven children who reached maturity, five of them suffered some sort of nervous disorder. The most fascinating character among them was Henrietta Emma Darwin, who was affectionately called Aunt Etty.

The family would sing a little song, composed by one of her nephews, at family gatherings; it sums up her charms.

> Question: *Fussy people Darwins are,*
> *Who's the fussiest by far?*
> Answer: *Several aunts are far from calm,*
> *But Aunt Etty takes the Palm.*

When Etty was only thirteen years old, she suffered a cold with high fever. The doctor recommended she ate breakfast in bed for a while, and Etty never again had breakfast out of bed. Ever since, she lived obsessed with her body and its complaints. According to her niece Gwen Raverat's memoir, Aunt Etty made poor health her primary interest and full-time occupation. She would write letters to her mother, Emma, detailing each of her symptoms, and she lived like a true invalid, with aides who helped her do every routine task. After lunch, she would have the cook come and count the plum pits on her plate, since she considered it to be of vital importance to her health to know how many she'd eaten. She also insisted her personal assistant cover her left foot with a silk scarf when she was sleeping, because she said it was always chillier than the right one. When it was cold season, she would wear some sort of gas mask she herself had invented. It was nothing more than a metal colander with cotton drenched in eucalyptus oil and some rubber bands that held it behind her ears. She seriously debated politics with her visitors while wearing it, unaware of the mocking her device elicited. And despite that obsession with her supposedly ill health, and her constant complaining, Etty lived to be eighty-four years old.

Like Darwin, I am obsessed with my children's health, but I am also aware of how my obsession could turn them into modern-day Etties. Anxiety disorders circulate widely within families. In fact, according to studies, close relatives of those affected are five times more likely to suffer from an anxiety disorder than the general population. And hypochondria is one of the most contagious habits.

In the case of the Darwin family, this tendency has been attributed to Emma Darwin's caring nature. It seems that in the Darwin household being sick was a noble distinction, perhaps because of the adoration the children felt for their father and their tendency to imitate him, but also because it was a pleasure to receive their mother's attention. In the words of her granddaughter, Emma 'was like a rock to lean on, always devoted and unwearied in devising expedients to give relief, and neathanded and clever in carrying them out'. In turn, Darwin's hypochondria has been attributed to his relationship with his mother. The child psychiatrist John Bowlby, defender of the famous attachment theory, maintains in one study that Darwin's mother's death when he was only eight years old set off in him a morbid fear of illness, loss, and mortality. Mothers, their excessive presence or their absence, hover like a curse over the Darwin family.

Even though psychiatrists and neurologists have invested eons of their careers in the search for the anxiety gene, to date the results have been quite poor. Neither the studies on genetic association nor the whole genome studies have clarified the origin of anxiety. Psychological theories of hypochondria vary widely: an overprotective mother or a deep unresolved conflict are usually the eureka with which the psychoanalysts try to cure hypochondria on the couch. They also interpret hypochondria as a way of managing one's own inability, low self-esteem, or dependence. According to that theory, when hypochondriacs believe themselves to be ill, they receive the protection and attention they long for but feel they don't deserve to get for other reasons. At the same time, they believe they have their protector's captive attention, since no one would abandon a sick person. Thus they replace their feeling of uselessness for one of illness, and they can fail without feeling guilty. In the light of that candle, any psychologist would think that I am seeking in illness the justification for all my failings as a mother, and a way to distract my conscience, which knows I'm out playing at politics when my nipples should be in my children's mouths.

When Freud was studying hysteria, he observed how some women suffered pathologies that were impossible to diagnose while they were caring for their ill parents. These captive nurses were victims of an irresolvable conflict between the desire for freedom, on one hand, and the love for their parents and the values that society had projected onto them, on the other. Hypochondria was a way out of a situation they conceived of as ambivalent. Illness gave them an intermediate path: they managed to not succumb to pure depression, but they also weren't fleeing and breaking with their loved ones and their established roles.

Over time I come to realise that hypochondria, like so many things that surround me, is language. David, already nearly six, still occasionally calls me to the foot of his bed. He has woken up in the middle of the night and tells me he can't get back to sleep, that he is feeling poorly. He explains that he has a bit of pain, but he can't tell me where, because everything and nothing hurts. What most worries me are the words he says next: it's a different pain, I feel different. After I take his hand, caress him, and speak to him gently so he falls back asleep, I head to the sofa. I stretch out there, but there is no way I can get any rest, and it's only four in the morning. During the hours in which I await dawn, all sorts of possible illnesses circulate through my mind, a diagnosis for this pain and no-pain, for this feeling different. With the first rays of morning sun, I find a possible key. My son's pain is in his soul. Death has just entered his life with the disappearance of a family member's dog he had spent many hours playing with. And he doesn't know how to tell me, how to tell himself, that he is no longer the same, that something in him has changed forever, and the loss, in his voice, is that feeling different.

How many stomach aches hide childhood fears, a cry for help in the face of feelings for which we do not yet have a name. But growing up doesn't mean we master language. We learn to talk little by little each day but also, in a way, each wound takes some words from us. As I sat by my father's deathbed, with his hand in mine, listening to the death throes that were telling me he was leaving forever, I could barely mumble an 'I love you so much'. And I've always been known for my loquacity, my capacity for encapsulating ideas, for finding the exact word no one was expecting, yet when the doctor came in to record the time of death and covered him with a white sheet, when he asked me how I was, when he wanted to listen to me, I was only able to tell him that my stomach really hurt and ask him if he could prescribe me something for that.

8

During the golden age of puerperal insanity, Isabella Shawe, wife of the celebrated British author William Makepeace Thackeray, went mad. She was only seventeen years old when she met her husband, and they married a year later. Isabella was practically still a schoolgirl and a bit sickly, but in the first four years of their marriage she had already given birth to three daughters. According to the author's account, during her first birth, in 1837, there was a horrible atmosphere in their home. Both grandmothers were present and arguing nonstop. Even though Annie was born healthy and everything ended well, Isabella took a long time to recoup her strength. She couldn't manage to nurse the baby and she felt extremely dispirited. It only lasted a few days, a brief storm that soon died down, but over time it would become a first fateful sign.

Soon after, Isabella would have another baby girl, Jane, this time in a much more placid birth. But the baby contracted a respiratory infection and died at only eight months. All that remained of her was a drawing made by Thackeray himself, depicting her on her mother's chest, and a malaise that Isabella didn't seem to want to relinquish.

A few months later, Isabella was pregnant again. As the birth approached, Thackeray described her as depressed, remembering the difficulties surrounding Annie's birth and Jane's death; the family's financial hardships weighed on her, she felt despondent over the state of her home and her mother-in-law criticised her inept housekeeping. The baby, a girl named Harriet, was born in the late spring and Thackeray felt exultant. As he would write to his mother a week later, 'the two small patients are getting on very well'.

But, by August, it was Isabella who would warn her mother-in-law that things were not going fine:

> I feel myself excited, my strength is not great and my head flies away with me as if it were a balloon. This is mere weakness and a walk will set me right but in case there should be incoherence in my letter you will know what to attribute it to ... I think my fears imaginary and exaggerated and that I am a coward by nature.

These are the only words we have from Isabella about her madness, which months later was labelled a disorder of postpartum melancholy with episodes of mania.

To try to cure her, the Thackerays set off on a voyage to visit Isabella's mother in Ireland. During the winding journey, Isabella gradually lost her bearings even more, until one day she threw herself into the sea and wasn't discovered for twenty minutes: she floated on her back in a vaporous white dress as she paddled with her arms. To keep her from further attempts on her life, Thackeray tied himself to Isabella with a ribbon around the wrist as they slept.

According to her husband, she would never recover her sanity. He concluded that she was 'God abandoned'. At first he paid her a lot of attention and continued trusting she would be cured: 'My wife will get well, I hope and believe.' But Isabella showed no signs of improvement.

> There is nothing the matter with her except perfect indifference, silence and sluggishness. She cares for nothing, except for me a little ... She is not unhappy and looks fresh, smiling and about sixteen years old. To-day is her little baby's birthday. She kissed the child

when I told her of the circumstance, but does not care for it.

Although for some time Thackeray tried to take care of her himself, Isabella ended up living in various asylums. Thackeray finally lamented in a letter to his mother: 'O Titmarsh Titmarsh why did you marry?'

Isabella's occasional improvements were followed by relapses and, over the years, all hope vanished. Her madness took on strange forms, like when she refused to let anyone leave the room, convinced they would never be able to return. In the letters Thackeray wrote to his mother, he explained that, in her brief moments of lucidity, Isabella claimed she'd been driven mad by guilt, her ineptness as a woman and as a mother, all her weaknesses.

Thackeray ended up referring to her as 'my dear little patient' and deciding that it would be best for them both if they never saw each other again. In 1848, the writer declared she was 'dead to us all'.

Isabella remained institutionalised until her death in 1893, fifty-three years after they found her floating in the sea. Her daughters and her grandchildren would visit her often. Her first-born, Anne Thackeray Ritchie, a novelist, was there at her deathbed: 'Her dear face lighted into serene and unspeakable wisdom and knowledge. It seemed to me that the room was full of light,' she wrote, recalling it.

Like Isabella, although not in words, I confessed to my mother-in-law, to the entire world, that 'I am a coward by nature'. I know that all this, the constant excessive reactions to every symptom, are fodder for my weakness. And I believe that Tomàs thinks he never should have had children with me, that the terrible words he spoke to me in the winged chariot were saying exactly that, if only he had never met me, if only he had never decided to perpetuate the species with someone like me. That I am also like a sixteen-year-old girl, immature and incapable of taking care of myself. How will I be able to take care of my children? 'Mortals ought, you know, to beget children from some other source, and there should be no female sex,' laments Jason to Medea, and if there is a woman who now deserves those words, she answers to my name.

In the early twentieth century, British psychiatrist Henry Maudsley encouraged husbands-to-be to scrutinise their fiancées for 'physical signs ... which betray degeneracy of stock ... any malformations of the head, face, mouth, teeth, and ears. Outward defects and deformities are the visible signs of inward and invisible faults which will have their influence in breeding.' The blame doesn't fall solely on me, I think, and I'm already absolving myself again. It was also Tomàs who, in that dimly lit club on Midsummer's Eve, didn't look closely enough for the signs of my insanity, and who was blinded by love into ceding to my whim to have children. And now that whim has muscles and tendons, and cries, and its life is a question mark that crushes me.

We know little about Isabella beyond her madness. It is said that in Les Thermes, the rural area on the outskirts of Paris where she and Thackeray honeymooned, her carefully trained voice and magical singing were remembered for a long time among those who heard it. Thackeray drew several portraits of her during the first months of their courtship. She was slender, ginger, with delicate features and an air of extreme shyness.

In one watercolour, she appears with her hair pulled back, a long neck, and an amount of clothing disproportionate to her tiny figure. She seems tranquil, her hands clasped in a sign of serenity. Only in the background of the painting do we see dense clouds that seem to presage the storm hiding in her soul.

My entire life I've been described in similar terms. It seems my appearance conveys a peace I do not feel. Perhaps it is due to my ghostly pallor, or the length of my arms and fingers, which gives me a languid air. If you don't know me very well, you might not notice those heavy clouds that also follow me, ready to release a torrential downpour at any moment. What does stand out, and I doubt anyone could miss it, is my stubborn proclivity for looking at the ground, which has gradually given me some sort of hump that during those first months of motherhood weighed on me more than ever.

The Renaissance doctor Giovan Battista della Porta was convinced he could discover the human soul through physical appearance. In the immense treatise titled *De humana physiognomonia*, he analyses in detail every physical trait and establishes numerous equivalences for each in terms of defects and virtues. And the worst of all, the trait that reveals the most petty and mean-spirited soul, is the hump. Because in the case of hunchbacks, he says, the flaw is near the heart, the beginning of the entire body. The best example of this is Thersites, a soldier in the Trojan War, whom the *Iliad* describes as a repulsive being who impertinently stands up to the powerful and who cravenly abandons the war to return home. For that, Ulysses hits him with his sceptre right on his hump, making him even more hunchbacked, and a fat tear slips down his cheek, while the rest of the army mocks him in unison.

One morning I am strolling through my neighbourhood particularly hunched over. On waking I'd found a red stain on my knickers, a sign my menstruation was returning. But I'd already started to overthink it and to entertain a thousand hypotheses far from that most likely one. Any change in my body upsets me, and I went out onto the street like Thersites, my head bowed, not wanting to see anyone, curved by the blows of hypochondria and determined to flee my body and the war that pits us against each other.

As I walk towards the market I pass Clara, a neighbour who lives at a psychiatric centre during the week. When she is at her parents' house at the weekends, she wanders the streets. Clara is a sort of mirror that reflects what could have happened to me if I had crossed certain lines, even though I don't know what those lines were in her case. She must be about my age, she grew up in the same squares, and she always tells me that she loves art. But for some reason she ended up institutionalised five days out of every week. She says that she lives in prison, and when I once asked her why she was there, she told me that she got mad at her clients too often. The clients are the passersby she tries to sell her drawings to. Every time she sees me, from a distance, she calls out my name and says, 'Nobody's buying.' She knows that I always do, and I have a folder filled with her creations.

Today, however, Clara doesn't greet me with the usual euphoria. Her expression seems more like mine, worried and contrite. When I reach her she whispers in my ear: 'Something happened to me.' We sit down on a bench and then she explains that a little bit of blood came out of her vagina. The coincidence concerns me, but I recover quickly and don't show it, because Clara is extremely frightened and for a moment I manage to forget about myself. I tell her it must be her period, and not to worry. She answers that she doesn't have a period. 'I don't have that. Or ovaries, or a uterus, or any of those things you have. I have nothing here,' she says as she points to her belly. 'That's why I can't have children like you do.'

Cotard's delusion, defined by a neurologist of the same name in the nineteenth century, occurs in cases of acute melancholy, when patients suffer nihilistic deliriums that make them believe they have lost their internal organs. Today it is mostly seen in cases of extreme hypochondria. That was the case for a woman known as Madame N., who, in 1888, right after the death of her baby from meningitis, entered a delirious phase and claimed not to have a heart or lungs. In her medical records, the psychiatrist described the torture her empty body caused her:

> She has no heart, she has no lungs, she no longer breathes and, as such, is immortal! Such an existence is impossible. This is her proof: no breath, no life, no death! She would be happy if she could die; ah! but she cannot, she is condemned to the impossible: always

feeling an impossible suffering. Her suffering will last forever, forever! They will never end; an hour will last billions of years and never pass.

Perhaps Clara suffers the same syndrome as Madame N., perhaps the three of us are linked by a runaway anxiety that has made us lose all logical perception of our bodies. But Clara's terror at the menstrual blood, her denial of its mere existence, reminds me of something else and makes me curse the world Clara was born into and of which I form an active part.

In 2020, when I'd been an MP for nearly five years, we voted in a plenary session for the end of forced sterilisations, which mostly affected women, many of them with mental disorder diagnoses. Every one of the parliamentary groups without exception voted in favour of ending them. Until then, in Spain, a judge could decide to sterilise a person with intellectual incapacities, without their consent. There was a policy of mutilating women's bodies that was totally legal. There were many MPs that day, in the halls, on the benches, who were surprised and said: 'Was that really happening?' 'How atrocious!' When I hear them say those things I will remember Clara, and how I put two and two together as we sat on that bench, how I soon learned that it wasn't that her organs had disappeared, as Madame N. complained, but that a judge decided to have them removed. I will remember how I could only tell her not to worry and that she should talk to her family or her doctors. How I went home to my children and left her sitting there, wondering what that red stain on her knickers was, since she doesn't have 'that', and how she didn't sell me a drawing that day and I didn't think to ask her for one.

From my entrance to Parliament in 2015 to the day that marked the end of forced sterilisations, there were 396 cases. In the press I will read about the case of a sterilisation that was about to be decided but was stopped by the implementation of the new law. It would have been number 397.

Jaume tells me I have an addiction I was unaware of; I'm addicted to certainty, he says, and he makes me see how I use the language of an addict. When I violate the rules I've imposed on myself and pounce on the computer to look for the symptoms I believe I or my children have, then I swear amid tears that I won't do it again, that this time is different. When I beg my family to listen to my worries, to come with me to the doctor, I promise them that this time will be the last. And like those mothers in the documentaries from the 80s lamenting having given money to their kid for their last fix, my mother, Tomàs, or my sister, sometimes gives in to my pleading. But Jaume has repeatedly warned me that, like a junkie, I will only get a short period of peace before the craving returns even stronger, because I will keep on slow dancing with death, as we all do.

I explain to him that I don't really think I'm crazy, that it is other people who are, those who ignore death, oblivious to this dance we are condemned to. They are the ones who live with an alienation that makes them ignore how disaster could strike at any moment, to us or someone we love. How can we laugh, how can we rest, amid this immense sinister dance?

In his chronicles, Greek historian Herodotus writes of how the Trausi, an ancient tribe of the Balkans, would sit around each newborn in a circle and weep for the woes it will have to suffer for having been born into this world. They would enumerate all the ills of human existence: the hardship, the pain, the disease.

I tell Jaume that as soon as I became a mother I understood the Trausi and their pragmatism. It's true that I've been aware of the existence of my mortality and illness even as a little girl. I was precocious and would obsessively question my mother on the subject. I would conjecture and calculate how many years of life I had left: in my child's mind no one got to a hundred years old, and so I would subtract my age from the ninety-nine I aspired to live to. At night, I would anxiously ponder the infinity of existence and, even more anxiously, its finiteness. But that fear of death's reality was somehow lighter because it only affected me. Now I want to protect my children from anything that could cause them pain, and that includes my own disappearance, which would condemn them to a motherless existence.

Jaume tells me stories. He explains one about a young Persian gardener who sees Death gesture to him at a market. Scared, he asks the prince to lend him his horse so he can flee to the nearby town of Isfahan to elude Death. The prince agrees and the young man gallops off. That evening, the prince meets up with Death and asks about the threatening gesture to the gardener that morning.

'It wasn't a threat, just surprise,' answers Death. 'I wasn't expecting to see him here, since I know that I must take him tonight, in Isfahan.'

What Jaume is telling me, with his stories and many hours of therapy, is that there is no way to escape death. No matter how often I palpate my chest, no matter how closely I observe my children, no matter if I turn my life and the lives of those around me into a hell, there is no mother, however strong she believes herself to be, however fierce she is, who can upend the rules of existence. All we can do is obey them and keep on living. Give our children love to offset the cruelty that may come, and raise them with the tools to best face up to it. He asks me to act, despite reality, he asks me for an act of will, of life.

Sometimes, the therapeutic duo made up of me and Jaume resembles the nineteenth-century philosopher William James. On one hand, James put action and will at the centre of his entire philosophy, and maintained they were the finest medicine against melancholy, and in that way Jaume is like him. On the other hand, his description of his neuroses could have been written by me: 'I remember wondering how other people could live, how I myself had ever lived, so unconscious of that pit of insecurity beneath the surface of my life.' It is often claimed that William James cured his severe depression without any medical attention; however, that isn't entirely true: he embodied both patient and doctor, a perfect combination.

Although he was born into an extremely privileged family, his talent and material abundance were shadowed by anxiety over many years. As a young man he suffered a severe crisis that nearly drove him to suicide. His depression was rooted in a contradiction that he found irresolvable: how to live in an insecure world when, in order to survive, you must act as if it were secure. At only eighteen years old, he drew a gloomy self-portrait in red pencil: a solitary young man seated with curved shoulders and bowed head. Over the figure, he wrote a phrase taken from Shakespeare's *King John*: 'Here I and Sorrow Sit'. If you look carefully at the handwritten inscription, you can make out a small erratum. Instead of an 'n', it seems James wrote an 'm'. Is it possible than instead of 'Here I and', James was going to write 'Here I am'? Was he already flirting with the self-affirmation that years later would save him from his sadness?

Only in his thirties did James manage to calm himself and find a meaning in life that lightened his anxieties. His biographers affirm that work and life were transformative.

He started teaching physiology classes at Harvard University and a publishing house commissioned the book that would become his monumental *The Principles of Psychology*. At thirty-six he married Alice Gibbens, who became a mainstay support against depression, as he himself acknowledged: 'Darling, in all seriousness you have lifted me up out of lonely hell ... You have redeemed my life from destruction.'

'My first act of free will shall be to believe in free will.' Those were the words that pulled him out of his depression, and this is the message Jaume is trying to convey to me. William James never completely got over his melancholy. It seems he often fled to the mountains, and it is even rumoured he visited healers who would release his sadness. Yet he chose optimism and action, and that gave him a worthwhile and useful existence. Sigmund Freud visited him a year before he died and said he hoped to be as brave and serene as James was when his time came.

When my session with Jaume ends, one of William James's most famous affirmations is echoing in my head: 'Be not afraid of life. Believe that life is worth living, and your belief will help create the fact.' The problem is I don't yet know how to put that into practice.

When I leave Jaume's office I usually go out onto the Somorrostro beach, which is right in front of the hospital. In the winter the tourists forget about it and, except for the occasional old person taking a cold dip as a tonic or someone walking their dog, I'm alone with the waves. I like to collect seashells, which can only be found in the off-season when the hordes of bathers haven't erased any trace of nature. Huddled over the sand, I fill my pockets, and the bigger they get the more treasure I feel I've gathered. Later, at home, I drill holes in them and run a thread through, wearing them around my neck proudly. They are the tusks of an elephant I've just hunted, the trophy for facing up to the beast that is my anxiety. And I amuse the babies with the necklace, with the melody it makes when I swing it in front of their little faces, cling-cling, clang-clang, and I move it from side to side to see if they'll follow it with their gazes. Here is a bit of the ocean and a bit of my anxiety, and it was I who gathered it up, for you, my children; I promise you I will calm this sea.

One day the plenary session runs overtime, and when I finally get to the hotel I realise I'm receiving a huge number of insults on social media. I soon figure out that someone has shared a photo of me in the session, sitting awkwardly and with my eyelids lowered. It looks as if I am taking a nap while the honourable members are debating. The photographs of politicians dozing in their bench seats are a whole genre. Any politician worth their salt has been betrayed by a still frame at just the moment they seem to have drifted off to fitful sleep. There is no use explaining that among the privileges MPs have is a comfortable sofa in each office; that far from the slavery of workers who cannot leave their job post, we are free to leave the plenary session if we fear we are nodding off. I have just made my grand entrance into the history of the genre with one of its finest masterworks.

From that moment on, I am the relentless victim of online bullying, and even some media outlets print the photo. Several people recommend I make a statement, but I don't have the heart. After all, the perception I have of myself isn't that different from the one shared by these legions of anonymous people who devote their free time to tormenting me. I would only like to tell them that they are incapable of besting me, because I am a champion of self-flagellation.

There is a famous photograph of Diana, Princess of Wales, sleeping sweetly at a public event. Dressed in a flouncy white and violet chiffon dress with satin trim, she looks like something out of a fairy tale. The snapshot is lovely, and it made its way around the world in the blink of an eye. But it didn't provoke the rage that my sleepy image does. Lady Di's subjects felt compassion towards her, especially after it was revealed, the following day, that she was pregnant. But blue blood does not run through my veins, and the sadism I incite gives me a very humble celebrity, far from that of a princess.

In private I receive displays of support from some colleagues. I would like to tell them I'm not bothered, that I'm too busy fighting against death, and that the only thing that worries me is my mother finding out. She has told me so very many times that I should sit properly, with my back straight, that I have to keep up my appearance, and she would suffer more than anyone seeing that her wise advice did no good. And we manage to keep her at a distance from that foul gale-force media wind, until someone sends the photograph to one of the group chats on her phone. She writes me that night. 'I've seen it. You can stop hiding it from me. It's okay. But you need to get more rest.' The avalanche of slander is so crushing and my posture so bad that even my mother is doubting my ability to stay awake during the day. I don't do anything to convince her either. I tell her I will do as she says and that I'm going to bed.

Needing to know is a scourge that sometimes destroys lives, Jaume tells me. There is no cure possible for someone who refuses to accept that uncertainty is a part of existence. And in my case, love was the first victim of this phobia of doubt. I know that Tomàs and I have come to a point of very difficult return. I've embittered a time that should have been lovely and which, with all the bluntness of cliché, we can never get back. Because, even though I try to conceal it with my victimhood, this lack of joy I've chosen can never affect just one person. If I've learned only one thing since becoming a mother, it's that there is probably nothing that is purely individual, and the domino effect of my anxiety is leaving corpses in its wake that I refuse to look at. But this silhouette on the ground that is our failed relationship will become increasingly hard to ignore. The shared perspicacity that brought us together will sooner or later have to admit that we must separate, that our love lost out to the black dog of anxiety.

One of the saddest love stories in philosophy was also caused by a stubborn melancholic, Søren Kierkegaard, who broke off his engagement to his beloved Regine. 'A depressive should not torment his wife with his suffering, but must act like a man and keep it to himself,' he recognised years later, considering himself condemned to never marry. And, at the same time, Regine begged him not to leave her, to let her remain by his side, sharing his pain. 'I will be eternally grateful if you let me stay with you and live in one of the closets of your house,' she begged, probably devastated. But Kierkegaard did not give in. They say he decorated one room with a tall wardrobe that he designed himself, of beautiful red wood, which resembled a standing coffin and was the last vestige of that love murdered by his melancholy.

One morning, David smiles for the first time. While I hold him in my arms, seated on the sofa, in some sort of drowsy state, he stares at me like an idiot with an unmoving smile. I'm disconcerted. I had imagined the crying, but I never thought the laughing would ever come. I smile back at him. When he was born, people soon began to say that David looked a bit like me, particularly because of our gigantic mouths. From the beginning I desperately hoped he would never be like me, hoped that instead I would dissolve and end up like him, hoped that David could change me entirely. But the truth is we share this huge mouth that now curves into smiles. And everything is suspended. This smile is the vine and fig tree beneath which I want to sit forever.

The reality of my children is overwhelming. I think that is what scares me. I, who was a wasteland, have created two undeniable facts. I, who had imagined, analysed, theorised about motherhood for years, am frightened by its materiality. I conceived the idea of being a mother as something abstract, a life project, a model of family, even a political venture. And amid crying, nappies, and pumping, I've discovered a viscerality that terrifies me, that is too much for me, that resists reason, that upturns any predictions, that subverts all planning. There is an immediacy in the role of mother that I've never been good at; I hesitate, I get flustered, and more and more awkward.

The person who lived beside the flat in London where Sylvia Plath committed suicide said he often saw Plath struggling with incompetence, which I also feel characterises me: she clumsily pushed an enormous old pram while holding another child by the hand, always with bags of rubbish or shopping, never able to keep up with it all. Plath soon learned that abstraction can be a threat to the cogency of life. 'The abstracts hover like dull angels', she says in a poem starring her daughter Frieda:

For her, the heavy notion of Evil
Attending her cost less than a bellyache,
And Love the mother of milk, no theory.

My identification with Sylvia Plath has gone through several phases. As a teenager, like so many others, I idealised her madness. We both felt that great muscular owl on our chests, gripping our hearts with its sharp talons, and I glimpsed in her a talent that we shared. Reading her journals made me aware of her descent into hell, and that her madness, even though it may have contributed to boosting her creativity, was a curse that no body of work can justify. Rereading her after becoming a mother, her journals, her letters, even the poems, brought me closer to a reality about which I hadn't heard much: her complex portrait of motherhood, both dark and luminous, and the honesty of a struggling mother who was probably led to her death by a feeling of abandonment.

In many of her poems, Sylvia Plath describes the intense love of a mother for her children and, at the same time, confesses that the attention they demand is exhausting. Her verses blend the ecstatic happiness of motherhood with descriptions of an unsettling nightmare. She just as easily sings a lullaby in an idealised atmosphere as she confesses an impossible longing for protection in a petty world where everything is threatening. 'A 10 day misery', she records in her journal when describing the birth of her second son,

Nick, and a month later she writes that having children is the best experience of her life. Plath transforms motherhood into a fertile territory where she confesses female anxieties, and this makes her a tremendously political poet, one who breaks with the stereotypes about what it is to be a mother while revealing the private sphere within the public realm of literature at a time where only men were allowed that privilege.

I read Plath's maternal narrative as if it were a Gothic novel. In her journals she details her recurring nightmares of giving birth to monstrous, blue, deformed babies. In her poems there are caves, crows, and piranhas.

Black bat airs
Wrap me, raggy shawls,
Cold homicides.
They weld to me like plums.

The bodies of the pregnant are haunted houses. Mothers wander through underground passages by night, and their words are beacons that illuminate the dark corners of the maternal mind, the terrors, the guilt, the contradictions. The world is a claustrophobic winter.

There is something Victorian in Plath's poetry, in those candelabra and dressing gowns with which she attends to her children in the middle of the night, in that fear an overactive imagination could harm the foetus, that terror of dissolving and getting lost forever in her maternal identity. Plath's poetic voice could have been that of one of those women driven at dawn to British asylums and diagnosed with puerperal insanity. In fact, Plath was writing at a historical moment that saw a return to the same feminine ideal of the Victorian era and sent women back into the domestic sphere under the stereotype of the angel in the house. After World War II, the thousands of men coming back from the front wanted the jobs that in their absence had been filled by women. Also, in a time of peace, heavy wartime industry was no longer necessary and they had to find another use for it. So there was an investment in clean lines and modern, efficient homes. In order for everything to fit together, doctors, politicians, businessmen, and publicists joined forces to convince the female gender that its biological destiny was motherhood, and that women's happiness and true power were hiding in the house of their dreams.

Betty Friedan, in the feminist classic *The Feminine Mystique*, published two years before Plath's death, shows how this cult to domesticity, this return to the home and to self-sacrifice, produced a profound malaise in an entire generation of women. Friedan names this abstract feeling 'the problem that has no name', a discomfort that could remain a mild but constant dissatisfaction, or could turn into insanity. Sylvia Plath not only had to live in this moral atmosphere, but also had to face the collapse of her ideal home.

Following her separation from her husband Ted Hughes, Plath assumed total responsibility for her children, both emotionally and economically, with her family on another continent. The overwhelming weight of motherhood was added to the pain of their divorce, in what was a particularly fragile moment for her. Some of her texts show her struggle to keep her children far from her desperation.

> *Your clear eye is the one absolutely beautiful thing.*
> *I want to fill it with color and ducks,*
> *The zoo of the new,*

she exclaims at the start of the poem 'Child', but the last verses admit defeat:

*Not this troublous
Wringing of hands, this dark
Ceiling without a star.*

In the final months of her life, Sylvia Plath was constantly crying out. Alone with her children, she moved to London, where she had to deal with months of snowstorms, power outages and the most intense cold the city had suffered in more than a century. Sylvia fell ill with a nasty flu, and the children had colds and coughs, one after the other. She refused her mother's offer to take her daughter Frieda to the United States as she was convinced that staying with her would be best for the girl. But in her correspondence she often repeats how she needs a nanny and how she fears she has lost her identity beneath the avalanche of responsibilities.

It would be unfair to not mention the joy and affection with which Sylvia treats her children despite the difficulty of the moment. A few months before her suicide, she tells her mother that she took the children to the zoo, that they put together a jigsaw puzzle, that she read them stories and they had a very fun day. I am sure that, just like me, Sylvia was capable of feeling sparks of absolute happiness with her children. Her penultimate poem, 'Balloons', explains a domestic scene of a mother and her children playing with the colourful balloons that remain in the house after the Christmas celebration.

*Such queer moons we live with
Instead of dead furniture!*

The mother watches the little boy and is surprised and delighted by his exquisitely different way of being, how he observes the world with wonder. It is a vitally alive poem that illuminates the joyful surprises motherhood brings.

Only nine days after writing it, Sylvia Plath commits suicide. So much has been written about her death that I don't feel like adding anything. All I will say is that, right before entering the great abstraction that is death, Sylvia leaves two glasses of milk on the children's bedside table, ready for when they awaken.

9

Party platforms do not usually have many measures for mothers. Except when wanting to control, prohibit, or foster it endlessly, politics has turned its back on motherhood. My parliamentary group, however, proposes a law that from the very start causes a commotion: making maternity leave and paternity leave equal and, furthermore, untransferable. The idea is that men will no longer be able renounce their paternal responsibilities, thus making childrearing more symmetrical, while also putting paid to the burden that weighs on women of childbearing age in the labour market, so that none of us is ever again plagued by the most inopportune of questions in a job interview. It is one of the first laws we want to put forward and, as a member of the Equality Commission, I am one of those responsible for it and am often an authority figure in meetings with groups of mothers. Meanwhile I have the father of my children chained to their cribs as I cross the desert every week to twenty worlds away, and yet I'm unable to let go of the heavy guilt I feel every time I see a pram on the Gran Vía and think about how I am not pushing my children's. The objective of these meetings is to understand mothers' views about the new legislation we are proposing, to defend it, and to seek a consensus I haven't even achieved with myself.

When I attend these meetings, usually held in one of the magnificent rooms of the Parliament building, I spruce myself up so I feel more confident. I put on clean, shiny shoes, in which, if I were to look carefully, I could see the hesitation in my pupils reflected, and I walk briskly to the room. But always, before entering, I am overcome with a feeling that I am barefoot, walking on stone, and time and again I lower my gaze. When I open the door, the rusty lock bolt whines due to a wind that seems to blow in from the past.

Sometimes I meet with fervent opponents of the law, collectives that defend the existence of a special biological bond between mother and baby. They demand the government respect and facilitate the development of this umbilical cord that, while not visible, they are certain exists and certain they know what it's composed of. So they demand longer leave for mothers than for fathers, and they offer as proof the psychological and physical damage produced by infants being separated from their mothers who go back to work. They cite all sorts of scientific studies and the terms 'attachment' and 'bond' spring from their mouths with a conviction that is a bullet to me. They know the names of every hormone and phase of child development, they have an itinerary covered in arrows, protecting them from this quicksand that traps me. Other collectives insist on the need for the state to put mechanisms into place to help mothers return quickly to work, so they can shatter glass ceilings. They are associations of successful female executives and business owners, who wear impeccable pantsuits and speak with astonishing confidence. They defend female leadership and strive to take over management boards; they often refuse schedule reductions or unpaid leave because they consider them obstacles in their ascent to the capitalist heavens. The behaviour of a single mother, according to them, has the power to undo years of hard-won feminist struggle. These are usually tense meetings, which – before the formal start – always and without exception begin with us chatting about our children to relax the atmosphere and to feel legitimised to participate in the discussions that will follow.

On one occasion when I'm not in the mood to flaunt my credentials, I distance myself from the circle of attendees who are arriving. I grab a heavy pitcher of water, lean towards its weight and fill the glasses so everything is prepared. Behind the spongy sound of my footsteps I hear a racket that comes from outside, encumbered, echoing like a thousand chariots pulled by two thousand horses about to enter battle. I look out the window to see where the sound is coming from and, in a leaden sky, the clouds trace the outline of hundreds of locusts with pointy stingers on their tails. From their crowned heads emerge lion's teeth that threaten to eat up every tree in the immense Retiro Park in the blink of an eye, and leave all of us gathered here without air. The pitcher suddenly crashes against the floor and glass shards scatter over the ancient carpet like sand in a tornado. Only then do I realise my hands are trembling at an unusual speed and that all the mothers are staring at them, shocked. When I manage to react, I leave the room with the excuse of getting someone from maintenance to clean up the mess. Instead, I take refuge in the toilet until my hands regain their usual serenity. I pull myself together and return to the meeting. But my anxiety does not go away. I think about the mothers who are beyond these rooms, so deprived of everything that they can't even set foot on the glass-covered floor of this building, so left out in the cold that they are completely defenceless against the flittering wings of the rabid locusts.

When the meeting ends, I remember Medea. I try to imagine how she would live after killing her children, if she was ever able to forget the screams of Mermerus and Pheres for even a moment, if she ever again felt a wisp of happiness. According to tradition, she fled to Athens, where she married and even had a son, and together they again left in a winged chariot to live out the rest of their lives together in what is now Iran.

Until Euripides's tragedy, in the Medea myth she was not the one who killed her children, but the Corinthians, in revenge for the murder of their king. It is believed the playwright changed the ending at the behest of the Corinthian authorities, who wanted to clear the reputation of their people. This change made it possible for Euripides to get inside the heart of a tortured mother, showing her pain and hesitation, her weakness and ambition. It wasn't the only time he would do that. In his works, Euripides showed with horrific clarity the dilemmas facing mothers raising their children in a man's world. In Ancient Greece, women had little freedom and few legal rights, they were nearly invisible and useless outside their homes. Even wise men of the stature of Aristotle and Galen denied that women contributed anything to the creation of children: it was the father who provided the seed of life, while the mother was just inert matter that held it within her for a while. That was the justification for women not having any right to the fruit of their wombs, which belonged, like all other possessions, to the father. Motherhood was so invisibilised that the birth most frequently represented in Ancient Greek iconography is that of a man, the all-powerful Zeus. The myth explains that the king of the gods had been warned that if his wife, Metis, gave birth to a girl, her second child would be a son who would overthrow the throne. When Metis was pregnant and about to give birth, Zeus swallowed her to outsmart the prophecy. Later, he was strolling by Lake Triton when he got an agonising headache and began to howl so loudly it could be heard throughout the firmament. His son Hermes ran to his aid and split his head with an axe, whence sprang Athena, armed and ready for war.

In a world where the most venerated birth is from a man's head, many have wondered what led Euripides to feel such an interest in mothers, when their role was so obscured. Little is known about his life, but it is said that he was extremely unlucky. He apparently was born and died in exile, had unhappy marriages, and his literary success did not stack up to his ambitions. They say that he had great artistic sensibility and was also a painter. Antiquarians of later periods believed they found artworks by him in the city of Megara. He was fervently opposed to being just one of the herd and he protested against moral norms, superstitions, and injustices. He died alone, far from his homeland and filled with pessimism and bitterness. Perhaps all of that led him to make mothers' misfortunes one of the central themes of his work. It seems that in order to understand a mother's misfortune, one has to have had a taste of their own.

Euripides was well versed in what had afflicted mothers over centuries, and what will continue to do so, surely, in the time to come. Because we not only have to face raising our children, supporting them and leaving them an inheritance in a world filled with insecurity. The gods can always inflict the worst of punishments, the death of your child, and then there is no possible consolation, as Euripides showed us in the lamentations of Andromache, in *The Trojan Women*. After Troy has lost the war against the Greeks and the Trojan women have been captured, they communicate to Andromache, widow of the slain hero Hector, that her enemies have decided to kill her young son. Before they throw him from the heights of the walls of the city of Ilion, his mother hugs him and says these words:

Oh to clasp thy tender limbs, a mother's fondest joy!
Oh to breathe thy fragrant breath! In vain
it seems these breasts did suckle thee,

wrapped in thy swaddling-clothes;
all for naught I used to toil and wore myself away!
Kiss thy mother now for the last time,
nestle to her that bare thee, twine thy arms
about my neck and join thy lips to mine!

After reading these verses, it is unsurprising that Aristotle deemed Euripides 'the most tragic of all poets'.

The first time taking my twins to the beach is a challenge that fills me with a pervasive melancholy over what my own childhood must have been like. I grew up in a city that lived with its back to the sea, and only when the Olympics were held there, when I was already reaching puberty, did it dare to face it. Fortune did not endow my family with sufficient capital to allow us a second home on the coast or those magical summers I always envied, filled with a loyal gang of friends and unforgettable first loves. I discovered the sea when, according to the psychologists, my traumas had already left their mark. I grew accustomed to fleeing there in search of consolation when perhaps it was too late for me to learn how to console myself. Which is why, one seemingly sunny Sunday, I feel I can't put it off any longer and I ask Tomàs to come with me and the kids to Barceloneta.

While we are on the bus, the sun gives way to a squall that threatens rain. But we continue on and cross the city to the Sant Sebastià beach, surrounded by palm trees and public swimming pools that, I can't help thinking, will inevitably succumb to rising sea levels in a matter of a few years. We leave the pram on the promenade, Tomàs picks up the girl and I the boy, and we walk out onto the surprisingly clean sand that's free of the usual summer litter. When we are near the shore I turn and, solemnly, show David the sea. The waves howl with the wind that's lifted, and white bubbly foam vigorously rises when they break. David grips my arms very tightly, turns his back to the ocean and bursts into a Herculean cry. I think he's afraid of that immensity spreading and that, just as the waves send spray everywhere, the chaos will hit us. I kiss him, speak to him gently, stroke him, hold him firmly in my arms and try to make him realise that the sea is his friend. I have to avoid any trembling in this foundational moment, which will remain in the deepest depths of his neuronal fabric all his life.

I was born in the century of Auschwitz and the Great War, of pop art and the avant-garde, of splendid cinema in grand theatres and the hole in the ozone layer, of nuclear energy and shrill modems, but it was also the century of scientific motherhood. The experts, in childrearing magazines and books with detailed instructions, dictated what a mother should do if she didn't want to set herself up as the guilty party for everything wrong with her child and, by extension, humanity. Psychoanalysis gave us suggestive names based on their primary defects. The freezer mother is one who wants to keep her child by her side forever, like an inert being devoid of free will; the crocodile mother, on the other hand, is the destructive cannibal who feels a love that knows no limits. At mid-century, Dr Winnicott, through his famous radio programme, wanted to liberate British mothers of all that anxiety. There is no such thing as the perfect mother, he told them, it was sufficient to be a 'good enough mother'. A sigh of relief was heard throughout the country, but it was short-lived, because if you didn't achieve that 'good-enoughness', if you had a moment of weakness, the psychosis was inevitable. While I try to hold David firmly, well clasped in my arms, I can still hear the words the old psychoanalyst addressed to hundreds of thousands of mothers swirling around the kitchen radio: 'If you have got a child's body and head in your hands and do not think of that as a unity, and reach for a handkerchief or something, then the head has gone back and the child is in two pieces – head and body; the child screams and never forgets it. The awful thing is that nothing is ever forgotten. Then the child goes around with an absence of confidence in things.'

I must hold David with all the firmness I do not have, and since I don't have it, I don't know if I'll ever be able to provide him with it. How can I explain that to a being who can barely stammer, who sees the Apocalypse in a wave, how can I ask him to forgive me for everything he will and won't be and, above all, how can I confess that I cannot promise him that I'll always be there to sustain him, that what he sees as a giant, the source of all his security, is nothing in the face of the laws of the universe. The arrow of time is inexorably drawing us closer to our separation with each passing second. The waves howl when I agitate the sea, I would like to tell him, but the reality is that its strength is due to the zig-zagging of the same serpent that decides the moment of our deaths.

Everything in this sea we observe is colossal. Its entrails hide thirty-thousand billion tonnes of salt, capable of covering the entire continent with a thick layer we could never escape. But beneath its foam there are also prodigious miracles and one of them can serve as a mirror for this new interweaving of lives that has me so uneasy. Coral, a nearly immortal animal which has built the largest known colonies of living beings, the architect of the oceans' brilliant colours, has created the most intimate symbiotic relationship in the entire animal kingdom. Without the singularly simple, single-celled algae called zooxanthellae, which inhabits the body of coral throughout its life, it would not be able to prosper. The reefs, with their fan-shaped radial symmetry, blooming flowers, striated brains and immense tubular organs, would not exist if these tiny algae and the coral polyps didn't make peace with their mutual interdependence.

Every once in a while, and with my help, David looks over at the immense blue. His fingers squeeze my coat, then relax, and every time he glances over he observes the movement of the waves a little longer. Sara, who is bolder, watches him with a warrior's air, comfortably installed in her father's arms. Some of the coral that hides beneath these tempestuous waters is tens of millions of years old. I would be content with living in symbiosis with my children for a mere lapse of that eternity. Since they were born, I've been trying to negotiate with death and with a God I don't believe in. Sometimes I surprise myself with 'I'd settle for eighty years'. Then I think I'm being too ambitious, and I lower it to seventy. But as I make those calculations, I realise it will never be enough, that the moment when that bond between algae and coral dissolves will always be a sword.

Gradually, imagining the algae and the coral polyps swaying in the ocean, I imitate their movement with my children in my arms, and observing Tomàs's happy expression, the four of us relax and enjoy a regular Sunday at the beach.

The atmosphere of group chats within political parties must be very similar to that of the underworld. A vapour comes off the phone screens and clouds your mind as if it were from Hell's fire; it batters your self-esteem and splinters your excitement and hopes. Since I entered institutional politics, one of my work tools is a Russian instant messaging app known for its security. The parliamentary group decided to create the chat on this platform because of its sophisticated methods of encryption, convinced they would keep anyone outside the group from getting in and reading even a syllable. What slipped easily through the encryption is hostility. When the euphoria of the first few weeks passed, along with the sudden affection between strangers it provoked, roles emerge and some of us are left with the less gratifying ones. Our debate spaces are almost desertic, our methods of working together on important decisions are reduced to ruins, although we've hardly used them. Information is the real treasure hidden in this house and not the works of art with famous signatures hanging on the walls, and it is much more elusive and easier to hide than impressive paintings. Soon it becomes clear that decisions are made in offices behind closed doors and in bars with plenty of wine and male bonding.

I assume without batting an eyelash that it falls on me to challenge these sorts of things, and to be the one who pulls out the abacus to count how few women are on executive boards and at important meetings. I am also the one who complains about the blackened filter through which information does not pass, keeping us in the dark as we go about our duties. But I am not the only one who has taken on a role. There are also those who remain quiet no matter what happens, those who close rank no matter what happens, those who are adulating no matter what happens, and those who confront anyone who doesn't take on one of those roles. And I become a target for the snipers. It does no good to limit my complaining to the confines of my home, far from journalists eager for discord. Also fruitless are the attempts to redirect the path that led us here: I am accused of high treason through emojis, rude blunt sarcasm +1.

One night, as I lie on the hotel bed, the debate among the parliamentary group turns particularly cruel. I defend a line of thought that, while not held by the majority, is supported by my regional federation. I oppose a centralism that has watered down the dreams of plurinationalism we held. Soon I become a shooting range where two of my female colleagues openly practice aim, while the rest of the participants watch silently. Aggression has free rein in this digital kingdom.

There is not much light in the room, nearly extinguished embers. Outside, snow has covered the streets of Madrid like wool and the greyish buildings illuminated by the moon seem like glaciers. Reading that succession of bullets, I falter, fantasise about scrawling my signature on a resignation letter and, with an automatism led by my fingers, I type 'in the name of mental health, I'm asking you to stop'.

When I reread what I've just written, a frozen fang punctures my hands. The claws that hold the phone loosen their grip, and it falls onto the bed. I start crying the way David and Sara do, with no brakes, a lonely sobbing that – again just like a baby – catches me completely by surprise. The snowstorm outside grows stronger and beats mercilessly against the window. I remain like that for a while, drowning out the sound of the wind with my crying. As my eyelids close, overcome by tiredness, the embers fading until the room is completely dark.

I am awakened by the buzzing of my alarm and, as I grab the phone to turn it off, I remember my words. I bring them to my dry mouth and they taste of regret. Not so much because they reveal my infinite weakness and my flirtation with madness, but because of the words I chose. There is something about the phrase 'mental health' that doesn't represent me. The whiteness of aseptic sanitary confines is not the colour of my suffering. There is nothing in those two words that attests to the delirium provoked in me the day before by the injustice. 'Delirium' was once classified as the behaviour of anyone alienated, no matter what the cause or origin. The word's literal meaning is 'to leave the furrow', which comes from one of the many tests that can be used to determine whether someone is mad: when you give them a stick to draw a furrow in the ground and they are unable to do it neatly, they join the ranks of those with 'delirium'. Yesterday I would have certainly been unable to trace a straight line in Madrid's white ground, and no scalpel for the soul would have changed that.

Today psychic suffering all falls under the medical category of mental health, and the so-called minor mental disorders are grouped into two categories: anxiety and depression. The first comes from the Indo-European root *angh-* meaning 'tight, constricted'. 'Depression', on the other hand, refers to a fall, like an atmospheric depression, with which we designate low-pressure zones that unleash gale-force winds and storms. Both terms have an indisputable negative connotation that is, in part, fair, because psychic suffering drags us down and confines us to narrow spaces. But at the risk of idealising pain, there is also an expansion when I am suffering, a kind of passion: my panic over death reminds me of the fight to be alive.

It was in the twentieth century when this new linguistic system around madness and the perception we have of it today was forged. As I was jumping rope under the burning sun of my city, a group of American doctors gathered to write the contemporary bible of insanity, the *Diagnostic and Statistical Manual of Mental Disorders*, better known by the acronym *DSM*. The impetuous expansion of the psychiatric pharmaceutical industry forced them to unify criteria in their diagnoses, since their practice was impossible without homogenous groups of patients for experimentation and medication. So they wrote up extensive accounts of symptoms, which the psychiatrist could check off as he listened to the patient's misfortunes, as if it were a shopping list.

It could seem like a simple advance in the modernisation of terms, but the consequences affect each and every one of us, those of us who live bound to madness but also those who believe themselves completely immune. No one any longer talks about the melancholy that Plato affirmed was related to the poet's 'divine fury'. There is no longer a creative force in madness, nor a compelling energy in sadness, nor rebellion in anxiety. The new terms blur and crush any ambivalences that melancholy has held throughout history and submit them to the reigning cult ideology of the free market. We depressives do not fit with the neo-liberal ideals of constant efficiency and positivity. As such, malaise relentlessly gains ground: the context in which we live produces depressives while at the same time excluding them. And here, in the face of this pain, the scavenging forces of the far right can make a killing. It is in the vulnerability and isolation we are confined to by a system that excludes us where those dealing in fear can gather their best harvest of profits.

After showering and dressing to attend the plenary session, I pick up my phone and open the chat of the parliamentary group. What a bad impression my words make. How exposed and useless they seem to me when I get to the part about mental health. I feel tempted to write asking them to forget what they've read. That I only wanted to appeal to reconciliation and shared ground. But I am also aware that I would still be unable to trace the furrow that would give me the composure to tolerate the chat's oppressive vapours; I decide to close it again and remain silent for a while.

My paternal family history is run through with madness. My grandmother fled, along with my father and his brothers, from a small town in Castile that condemned them to poverty. As their material conditions improved in a Barcelona that opened its arms to them, they each fell into depression. It would stay with most of them the rest of their lives, and I was an imitative witness. Whatever the hypothesis, nature or nurture, it is true that a vestige has reached me. The last thing in the world I want is to bequeath it to my children. I often say that to Jaume, asking him why my family had to succumb to suffering like that, I beg him to give me the keys to end this painful legacy. Jaume tries to make me see that not everything about what plagues us is negative: 'If it weren't for you, there would be no art,' he tells me.

In *In Search of Lost Time*, Marcel Proust recreates, with the story of the death of the narrator's grandmother, the death of his own mother. Doctor Du Boulbon visits her on her deathbed. The doctor is convinced her time has not come and that her ills are psychological. So he prescribes a stroll beneath the laurel trees on the Champs-Élysées and labels her a neurasthenic hypochondriac. When she protests, Du Boulbon gives a panegyric to neurotics:

> Submit to being called a neurotic. You belong to that splendid and pitiable family which is the salt of the earth. All the greatest things we know have come to us from neurotics. It is they and they only who have founded religions and created great works of art. Never will the world be conscious of how much it owes to

them, nor above all of what they have suffered in order to bestow their gifts on it.

In the desperation that imprisons me since my children's birth, I am unable to contribute to this splendid family, and anxiety blocks the impulse to write that sometimes overtakes me. But it is true that, in the moments of concentration I am able to snatch from my state, I get in touch with my mad ancestors. In some sort of literary Ouija, they are resurrected before me through their diaries, poems, and letters, and they manage to console me more than all the Pfizer employees put together. I most see myself in the medical records of those Victorian madwomen. I search out and voraciously devour their words. Each of their laments has a bitter taste, but as I work on this archaeological task of reconstructing the foundations of my insanity, I begin to feel a sweetness similar to honey.

Nineteenth-century Europe was witness to a vast increase in mental hospitals and inpatients. 'I doubt if ever the history of the world, or the experience of past ages, could show a larger amount of insanity than that of the present day,' bemoaned Dr John Hawkes, of the Wiltshire County asylum. Many of us today think the same thing when we see the overwhelming statistics on anxiety, depression, and psychosis from the World Health Organisation, which speak of veritable epidemics. Perhaps we and our ancestors from the 1800s share a mysterious virus that comes back every so often to attack us, perhaps we are victims of the same diagnostic bias that condemns all suffering to the vast sea of psychiatry, or maybe we are living the same tumultuous time that, as Dr Hawkes observed, demands 'higher standards of intellectual attainment, a faster speed of intellectual travelling, greater fancies, greater forces, larger means than are commensurate with health.'

As I open one book after the other, I learn the old languages used by my predecessors in pain to give voice to their fears. Madness has always, in every moment, had its vernacular, and Victorian patients often chose the language of religion, whose consolation and threat flooded quotidian life. The asylums' archives show that hundreds of them claimed distress over having transgressed God's will and lost their souls as a punishment. After all, if Satan exists and has even a minimum of perspicacity, he would know that there is no worse torture than a good panic attack. And I, a convinced atheist, find in their words more of a mirror than in those of the *DSM*. Like those of Ellen Penfold, a twenty-eight-year-old dressmaker with five children who stated that she was 'dead and turned into dust' and demanded God open up the bolted door to Paradise. Alice Mary Aphius, an inpatient in Essex County, always swore she was dead and had managed to slip into heaven despite not deserving to be there. When she entered the asylum, she confessed to having committed terrible sins, the worst of which was having turned her husband into a woman. I wonder what became of Alice and her suddenly female spouse, but all I find is that she was released soon after with a conclusive 'improved' as the final note in her medical record. One of my biggest unsolved mysteries features poor Eliza Miller, admitted after the death of her baby to Colney Hatch Lunatic Asylum, where she could only stammer out that she had committed 'the unpardonable crime'. A few days after her admittance, she slit her throat with a ten-centimetre knife. When they asked her husband for her birth certificate in order to expedite the death certificate, he responded by letter that he did not have it, since Eliza had burned a lot of documents before she went into the asylum. Sometimes at night I imagine Eliza, her haggard face illuminated by the bonfire she lit, and I wonder what she was trying to hide in the flames, what her crime was and if perhaps I could help her to find forgiveness.

As I attempt to contribute to a better world through politics, I can't stop savouring a pain that, I realise, is quite narcissistic. I can't help thinking that this escaping into the past, to other eras of madness, is a search for a justification of my cowardice and immaturity. There is also something fetishistic about this pleasure in affliction that is not fair to my children and could turn into paralysis. But at the same time I think that if we don't travel this saturnine orbit alone, perhaps we can give it a more complex meaning and turn it into political power.

In Parliament I am a member of the Cultural Commission and in the last few years I've also been its spokesperson. I am one of the few women who attend the sessions, which are dominated by grey neckties who too often use culture as a currency to placate the regional delegations of the parties. Seated in one of the spongy oxblood leather armchairs, I witness how the ascension of the reactionary parties has expanded even further the belief among politicians that culture is just an ethereal distraction, a leisure activity more suited to the wealthy classes than those with empty pockets. The Roman doctor Asclepiades of Bithynia treated his mentally ill patients by means of 'symphonia'. Today we fight for public healthcare in which everyone has access to their dose of serotonin in pill form, but we forget that art can be one of the best allies for understanding the meaning of our pain. Instead of silencing it beneath bewilderment, art can imbue it with transformative energy.

The president of the commission is an older man who looks a bit like Valle-Inclan, an old-school doctor, the kind with distinguished cultural baggage, who makes very erudite references in his addresses during the sessions. Discouraged by all the parliamentary work, I am exasperated by his endlessly long speeches, which seem oblivious to the infinite schedules of the MPs listening to them. One day, however, he catches my attention: rather than making one of his vehement affirmations, he poses a question for which he does not seem to have an answer. 'What is culture? I do not know, honourable ministers,' he laments, and as trite as it is, my empathy is aroused by his acknowledgment of doubt, something highly unusual in that setting, and it leads me to reflection.

Possibly the most precise answer could be found not far from that building, at the Museo Reina Sofía, in an exhibition of engravings by the German artist Käthe Kollwitz. Her dark works denounce poverty, injustice, and the deaths caused by starvation and war.

Kollwitz was witness and victim to two world wars, the first of which snatched from her one of her two sons, Peter. The second took her grandson, again piercing her heart, thirty years later. At the end of her life, the Nazis bombed her home and studio in Berlin. 'War will accompany me to the end,' she wrote when at death's door.

For me, Kollwitz has one of the qualities I most admire, and find most lacking in Parliament and in myself: her ability to change her mind, to evolve her ideology, to contradict herself over the course of a lifetime, as evidenced by the intellectual shifts she recorded in her diaries.

In 1914, like most Germans, Kollwitz accepted the war as a defence necessary for national survival. When her son Peter wanted to enlist in the army, she helped him convince her husband to give his approval. Before he left, she gifted him a bouquet of flowers and a copy of Goethe's *Faust*. After his death, her desire to honour him, to justify his sacrifice, kept her from condemning the war and its atrocities. Her diary entries reflect a fierce emotional and intellectual struggle: 'Is it a breach of faith with you, Peter, if I can now see only madness in the war?' she wrote in the midst of her own battle. Finally, pacifism wins out, and Kollwitz ends up committing to non-violence, which for her is 'not a matter of calm looking on' but rather 'work, hard work'. And Kollwitz's art was also that for her.

Only four months after her son fell in Flanders, Kollwitz wrote in her diary an affirmation of life and a possible response to the question all politicians must ask themselves regarding culture:

> Peter was seed for the planting which should not have been ground. He was the sowing. I am the bearer and cultivator of a grain of seed-corn. What Hans will become, the future will show. But since I am to be the cultivator, I want to serve faithfully. Since recognizing that, I am almost serene and much firmer in spirit. It is not only that I am permitted to finish my work – I am obliged to finish it. This seems to me to be the meaning of all the gabble about culture. Culture arises only when the individual fulfils his cycle of obligations. If everyone recognizes and fulfils his cycle of obligations, genuineness emerges. The culture of a whole nation can in the final analysis be built upon nothing else but this.

And in this cycle of obligations, Kollwitz used her art to denounce the appropriation of the maternal figure. Faced with the image of the woman who symbolises the nation and the power of sacrifice by offering up her brave sons, or the pregnant woman who represents the capacity for national regeneration, she paints black, energetic mothers who repudiate that infinite loss and place life above the lifeless ideal.

And that is what is represented by the circle of rage that is *Die Mütter* [The Mothers], part of a series of lithographs against the war that have become a symbol of feminism and the struggle for peace. It shows a group of mothers who huddle together to protect their children and convert the female duty of sacrifice for the fatherland into one of maternal solidarity. On the left, one of them covers a little boy's eyes, and I could swear she is trying to conceal her trembling so the boy doesn't perceive the frightened movement. On the right side, a giant arm embraces two women, one of them with the stunned features of the artist. The hands form intricate patterns, fighting to keep all the bodies safe from the violence outside the huddle. But what I like best are the long fingers, very long, and their unprecedented elasticity, able to create firm walls of bone, flesh, and skin.

Although I do not have an answer to the question posed by the president, although many MPs there believe they do, there is one thing that is clear to me. This tower of mothers is a good example of culture's reach, and strolling through this exhibit of dark hope that unnerves an entire room of the Reina Sofía, confronting those mothers' gazes, is perhaps the best policy-making we could do today in Parliament.

In my datebook, sessions with Jaume mix with meetings with ministers, organisations, and activists, and the references to laws and parliamentary initiatives are followed by notes about my anxiety. The amygdala, the insula, the hippocampus, the ventral striatum, the stria terminalis, and the anterior cingulate cortex. I adroitly write out these beautiful terms, as if somehow that would allow me to control them; they refer to the brain circuits involved in this hyperactivation of fear that is anxiety, and they function thanks to the famous neurotransmitters that my medication attempts to tame.

The nineties, the decade of my adolescence, saw the birth of the miracle Prozac and its siblings. It is called, not in vain, the decade of the brain. I grew up with these biological trappings, which also accompany me in these episodes of insanity. The imbalances that according to Hippocrates and his contemporaries were provoked by the humours, are now caused by dopamine, noradrenaline, and serotonin. They are resounding words, forceful in their scientism. But I know they are incapable of completely explaining the world's madness, and I know we won't find all the consolation we are seeking in their pills.

I don't believe the medication has any effect on my anxiety. I don't deny its virtues in certain circumstances, I don't refuse pharmaceutical alchemy and its ability to assuage pain. But I know that the roots of my suffering don't respond to their orders. I've accepted the treatment only as some sort of pact with the world: a commitment with those who surround me and just in case. The same just in case that made my grandmother go to Mass, as she herself confessed to me.

One day, when no one was listening to us, she explained that sometimes, standing there praying the Our Father in a chorus, she suspected that God did not exist, but in case he did, that time spent in church would give her a right to Paradise and would have been well invested. Today there are people who hang the structure of serotonin, that logo made up of hexagons and diagonal lines, around their neck, the way my grandmother wore a crucifix.

I go through life negating my body, so I reject any physical explanation for my malaise. But Jaume forces me to look under the skin, and makes me see that, by hating them, I've established such a close relationship with my viscera that they sometimes lead my anxiety. Each of our bodies is a concert, he tells me, and we constantly live with the background music played by the orchestra, without paying much attention. But I am the director of that orchestra, alert to the slightest imbalance, to whether that violin entered too soon, to whether the wind section isn't completely synchronised. And those are the stabs, prickling, pressure, burning sensations.

Anxious people, and particularly hypochondriacs, have a highly developed perception of our bodies. Psychiatrists have termed it 'visceral hypersensitivity', and the same phenomenon is produced in poor lab animals: subjected to constant torture, they can no longer stop feeling their bodies. Yet, on the other hand, anxious people are radically tolerant to pain. We moan and whine all day over the slightest sensation in our bodies, but we are able to withstand enormous amounts of pain without shedding a tear, and that also has a name: the 'anxiety paradox'.

One day, after heating up Sara and David's porridge, I pick up the grille that protects the stove burners when it's still hot. In that instant, I hear the same sound as when cattle are branded with a red-hot iron. I look at my hand, marked by the fire, and it gives off the smell of burnt flesh. Tomàs runs to my side, stunned, and tells me I have to go to the emergency room. But I shrug my shoulders, calm as can be. I say there's no need and I just start feeding the twins.

10

Visits to the paediatrician form part of the quotidian life of every infant's first few months. A high fever, eczema, strange colours or textures in their stool. Among the infinite moments of waiting in childrearing, there are those we spend in doctors' waiting rooms, punctuated by the coughs emerging from prams covered to keep viruses out, and surrounded by mothers who compete for who has the biggest, darkest circles under their eyes. At one point, already mid-spring, David runs a fever for a few days. Popular wisdom insists that children grow when their temperature passes thirty-seven degrees Celsius. I would swear that every day his eyelashes are longer, curling and nearing the heavens at a vertiginous pace. On the third day, the fever hadn't lessened and I show up at the doctor's office with those insolent lashes.

The doctor gives him a thorough checkup and, when checking his ears, she detects a slight inflammation indicating a harmless ear infection. When she lifts his shirt to listen to his chest, she notices a light brown birthmark on his ribs, beneath his left nipple. It is quite large for such a tiny body, and I'd seen it when he was first born but hadn't made much of it. However, just then, to ensure I have everything under control, I ask, 'That spot isn't anything ... is it?'

'No, that's a birthmark. There's nothing to worry about if he only has one. Does he have more than one?'

'No,' I respond.

I dress the baby and we leave her office with a prescription that promises to bring him back to wellbeing in a matter of a few hours. And it keeps its promise. That night, David no longer has a fever and he rests in his crib oblivious to the agitation that is about to overtake me in the bed beside him.

Because just as I am falling asleep, when my limbs and jaw finally relax, the doctor's words about that mark on David come back to my mind, in the form of a nightmare. There's nothing to worry about if he only has one. And that is where all the 'what if's that Jaume had warned me about begin to run riot. What if he has another one I haven't noticed, hidden in one of his infinite folds? What if he doesn't have another one today, but one appears tomorrow, or the day after tomorrow, or next month, or any of all his birthdays to come?

Since my family noticed that spot, they'd always tried to find a correlation between it and some food. An asparagus, long and with rounded edges, like those my paternal ancestors grew in Castilian lands, or a sweet potato, like those my grandmother baked for the day before All Saints' in her mezzanine apartment in Eixample and which I savoured. Finally, they opted for a less elegiac but more realistic choice: a chip, like those I devoured during my pregnancy and had to banish when the gynaecologist set off the alarm at my weight gain. In Antiquity it was said that if a pregnant woman craved a fruit or some other food and she touched a part of her body at that moment, its shape would be forever imprinted on the foetus's skin. There was a time when it wasn't only distant rural relatives and old lady neighbours who'd lived through a war who saw cravings in those marks; wise men such as Hippocrates, Aristotle, and Saint Augustine also defended their existence. In the sixteenth century, the German physician Daniel Sennert recorded horrifying testimonies of the power of maternal fantasies: a pregnant woman who witnessed a butcher chopping a pig in half gave birth to a baby with a palate cleft to its nostrils; another, who was feeding the livestock when she suffered an attack from a goose. She hit it with a stick and left it lame, only to give birth to a baby with a leg that vividly resembled the animal's broken one.

When I first saw David's birthmark, it looked to me like an island, clearly. A long, narrow island with welcoming geography and accessible coasts for a mother like me, lost in the ocean like a wooden splinter from a shipwreck. But suddenly, that night when David's ear infection lets up, I start to fear that his body is an archipelago, with myriad bits of land spotting his epidermis, pearly from the warmth of the heating. And, ignoring all the psychologist's instructions, I get out of bed to check on him for the nth time.

Through the window, the full moon illuminates the bedding I now brusquely push aside. And when observing his tranquil body, oblivious to the owls and rooks landing on the sill, I can make out an infinite number of spots that, surprisingly, I hadn't seen before. In a matter of seconds, the moon is dressed in blood red and no longer allows me to clearly see the outlines that were so well-defined moments earlier. With a trembling hand, I pick up my phone, turn on the torch feature and, as if it were an oil lamp, draw close to David. But my vision has clouded, my heart's beating increases frenetically, I feel the tickle of an army of ants marching over my body, and the vapours that emanate from my hypochondria, hot like an oven, turn into cold sweat on contact with my freezing skin.

When I fall into bed and my phone hits the ground, Tomàs wakes up and asks me what's wrong. I try, through sobs, to explain to him that an archipelago is growing on our son, and that the paediatrician had said that if he just had one spot, that was fine. 'If it was just one, you understand? If it was just one.' Tomàs goes over to the boy's crib, covers him up again and kisses him as protection against his mad mother who has just been scrutinising him and threatening his innocence. 'He's fine, trust me,' he says. 'Forget about it. There are no spots, there's nothing on him, he's perfectly fine. You have to make an effort to get these thoughts out of your head.'

In the seventeenth century a dispute arose between what were called the imaginationists, who believed that a mother's fantasies had the power to transform her child, and those who opposed that belief, the anti-imaginationists. The sage Ludovico Antonio Muratori, in his treatise *Della Forza della Fantasia Umana*, widely discussed both theories and, although he did not take sides, he did recognise that human imagination has a surprising strength, and particularly women's imaginations 'due to their vivacity and for other reasons'. Perhaps what these scientific debates concealed was a terror over the female capacity to conceive and give birth, and a desire to control maternal thoughts and keep them pure: 'do not leave room for such absurd concepts or thoughts, but rather avoid at all cost seeing or hearing these horrible objects or filthy spectacles,' Lluís Vives would say.

During my entire pregnancy I was afraid that my anxiety over everything turning out fine would have the opposite effect, that my fears and terrors would irrevocably damage the children. Even when you are trying to conceive, and particularly if you have fertility problems that rightfully concern you, everyone warns you that the more you wish for it, the more you worry about it, the less chance you'll have of success. No one seems to realise that this advice has the opposite of its intended effect. I remember being a sack of nerves, thinking I mustn't think that I wanted to get pregnant in order to get pregnant, and trapping myself in a psychological conundrum that barely let me get any rest.

And here we have it now, this island on David's torso, perhaps the unerasable mark of my uncontrolled ruminations, and again my thoughts threaten my children: I am capable of multiplying that solitary island, smothering my son with so much terra firma and depriving him of this calm sea that flows over his skin.

My exact diagnosis is generalised anxiety disorder with predominant obsessive thoughts. That means that I'm unable of escaping the cage I constructed myself, of the simplest material: a single idea on endless repeat. Over the last few days I've become the guardian of my son's body: I inspect its tones, in sunlight, artificial light, at every hour of the day and in every position. It doesn't matter that my mother insists bodies aren't smooth and my gaze is not objective, or that Tomàs swears that the spots I see are just the normal irregularities on every epidermis ... I can't stop checking.

One afternoon when I can no longer bear the sight of all those islands, I tell Tomàs that the paediatrician asked me to bring David back to check on his ear infection and, using that subterfuge, I free myself from the sanity authorities and head to the health centre. I have to explain to the doctor that I made a mistake, that I told her he only had one spot, but really there are hundreds, thousands, under these innocent clothes, and that only she and I are able to see the importance of them.

Once I've given the taxi driver the address, I immerse myself in some sort of communion with David, and I tell him with my mind that he shouldn't be scared. I hold him on my lap and he rests his head on my arm. Looking at his nape, I realise our flesh is exactly the same colour, that there is a kind of unbroken continuity. The taxi clatters along the asphalt as if we are in a carriage. David grips me tightly, and beneath his whimpers I think I can hear the sobbing of a woman who is not me. Outside grey buildings streak by, and in their stones I see the vestiges of a weeping mother. I remember the majestic dome of Santa Maria del Fiore, the grandeur of the Notre Dame cathedral, the humility and harmony of the walls of the basilica of Santa Maria del Mar, and the miraculously high bells of the Roman Santa Maria Maggiore. In their pealing I travel to chapels in hidden valleys, with tempera Virgins – inscrutable, symmetrical, and ubiquitous – who hold up the Baby Jesus. The three envelopes with apocalyptic news from the Virgin of Fatima. The pendant of La Moreneta my eponymous grandmother Montserrat always wore around her neck. The *Madonna del Prato*, the Virgin of the Rocks, of the Pomegranate, and of the Goldfinch, as seen on slides in a secondary school classroom. My aunt named Angustias after Our Lady of Anguish, and the legions of Dolors, Soledats, Esperances, Immaculades, and Encarnacions I've met throughout my life. The Angelus prayer at dawn; the Hail Mary my great-grandmother would repeat up to fifty times, dressed in strict mourning attire; that white marble with which Michelangelo sculpted a mother's worst nightmare. Bathed in the gleaming light that enters through Gothic stained glass with a female silhouette, I think of those cured by Our Lady of Lourdes, of those saved by the Virgin of Guadalupe; I'm reminded of the lovely embroidery worn by the Virgin of Hope of Macarena at the Andalusian House my mother would take me to as a little girl. I'm dazzled by a long shawl of lapis lazuli, carmine, and gold painted by the greatest masters, so great that within them the 'three times virgin' embraces all of humanity. The floor of the taxi fills with roses, lilies, and thorns, the moon moves to beneath my feet, my dress converts into the sun and a dozen stars crown my head. David caresses this Virgin of Tenderness who holds him. I am the Mater Dolorosa, alone and self-sacrificing, resigned to my fate of witnessing my child's suffering. I've accepted my fate and, as I get out of the cab, these two bodies that are one do not cast a shadow.

The historical foundation of the Virgin Mary is surprisingly fragile. Like so many mothers, history turns its back on her. In the Gospels she is only mentioned eight times, and her name appears on four paltry occasions. Mark and Matthew cite her without giving her much importance; John vaguely alludes to her presence in Cana and Calvary; Luke devotes just a fleeting passage to her, and Paul completely ignores her. But in the first century she emerged from oblivion in the apocryphal gospels. The myth of Mary was born to be an instrument, a mirror of a people tortured by war, illness, and death, in order to keep them selfless and self-sacrificing just like her.

I walk with trembling steps to the reception desk at the health centre and, when asked 'what's wrong with your son', I answer humbly: 'he has spots'. And I sit down to wait. While David's nails grow, along with his limbs, his teeth, his genitals, his hair, and his peach fuzz, I wait, sitting with my arms on my knees. But I don't know what I am waiting for, because I am not the owner of what is to come, and I find that unbearable.

When we enter the paediatrician's office, she looks at me in surprise. She doesn't remember that 'what if', she doesn't understand what I'm telling her about the spots. I get flustered trying to explain it, I stutter, sigh, and wave my hands in desperation. She seems more alarmed by my behaviour than by those spots that, wrinkling her nose, she says she will take a look at. After I undress the baby and hand him to her, I stand beside the examining table.

The sorrowful Mother stood
weeping before the cross
where hung her Son.

We don't know what Mary was doing while her son was captured, sentenced, and condemned. No Evangelist thought those things worthy of mention, but popular tradition supposes that she watched him for hours as he carried the cross to Calvary, was whipped by the Roman soldiers, and hung on the cross while still alive. When her son died, Mary's soul, 'his sorrow sharing, all his bitter anguish bearing', was finally, as the prophet told her, pierced by a sword. All those *pietàs* in stone, fresco, oil, and wood, in which the mother of us all holds her dead son, speak of pain, of loss, of absence, but most of all they speak of loneliness. I know that full well, as I stand here, the only possible font of the true reasons that brought me to this doctor's office. But other women accompanied Mary in her grief: her sister, Mary of Clopas, and the infamous Mary Magdalene. I search for them with my gaze, because if we'd given them a bigger role in this story, if their hands sustaining Jesus's body covered the altars of our world beside those of Mary, perhaps today, here, I wouldn't find myself so alone. But that would surely free us from the sentence the Mother of God represents and from that sword that has been piercing the heart of Western femininity for twenty-one centuries.

In most representations of the *pietà*, the mother is younger than the son. Because the Virgin is so pure that she doesn't even age. In fact, since she is free of all sin, her flesh does not decay and when she dies she goes up to Heaven with her immaculate, light body. I, on the other hand, after dressing my son and sitting down, as the doctor requested, am pure weight, sunk into this chair, I am wrinkles, dark circles, hump. The doctor tells me that David is fine, that he doesn't have any marks beyond the one I showed her the other day. She looks at me with a mix of stupefaction and empathy and asks me to calm down. I thank her and leave the office with my son in my arms. When I get out on the street, I note the taste of grass in my mouth and I feel not only crazy but ridiculous.

On 10 October 1517, at his last residence, the French castle of Clos Lucé, Leonardo da Vinci received the Cardinal of Aragón and his entourage. He showed them the notebooks written throughout his life and three paintings that were so valuable to the painter that he'd brought them with him from Italy: a Saint John the Baptist, the Mona Lisa, and a Virgin and Child with Saint Anne. This Virgin, which today hangs in the busy halls of the Louvre, obsessed Leonardo during his final years. So much so that numerous preparatory sketches and workshop versions have been found. The representation of Jesus with his mother and grandmother unsettled Leonardo. There was something in that portrait of three figures that was problematic for him, and he persisted in trying to resolve it until the end of his days. Unfortunately, the painting remains unfinished.

Before Leonardo's painting, the iconography of these three characters together was a series of rigid and dull patterns, lifeless images arranged in vertical or horizontal juxtaposition. But Leonardo didn't settle for those models. He wanted to show Mary's tenderness towards Jesus, and Anne's towards Mary, and the complex gaze of son to mother. And in his painting the horizontality and verticality become a pyramid that provoke a strange pleasure. The boy plays with a sheep, an ill-fated symbol of the sacrifice to come; Mary grabs him lovingly so he'll forget about that inauspicious toy and perhaps change his fate; and Anne holds her daughter on her lap and looks at them both sweetly.

I wonder what Leonardo wanted to convey with this soulful composition and those crags, which to me look like ice cream, in the background. Perhaps that Jesus is telling his mother with his gaze that she shouldn't worry, that he has accepted his fate and that there is serenity possible in the face of even the cruellest of life's vicissitudes. Or maybe he is telling her that he needs her, that he's vulnerable, and that there are dangerous games against which he cannot act alone. In turn, Anne's gesture explains to her daughter that she is also sustaining her, that she is her anchor when she leans towards her son to protect him.

The philosopher Adriana Cavarero saw, in this matrilineal continuum painted by Leonardo, a potentially infinite series of leanings, and a challenge to the rectitude imposed on us. The rigidity of that static, vertical tree to one side of the painting, represents the masculine ideal incapable of bending, even for love. Both Cavarero and I realise that this vindication of maternal leaning could perpetuate the portrait of the self-sacrificing, servile, always willing mother. But there is another possibility, that this leaning isn't based in instinct or gender, but in an ethical decision, a decision that means choosing caretaking over injury, peace over violence. Then, even the firmest tree and the pointiest crag would be capable of leaning in this gesture that stubbornly occupied Leonardo's thoughts until the day he died.

When I explain to Jaume the appearance of the spots and my furtive visit to the paediatrician, he tells me that I am focussing my efforts in the wrong direction. All the checking of David's skin and consulting the doctor I'm doing is designed to eliminate uncertainty, but what I should do is embrace it. No matter how many hours of effort I devote to it, no matter how much sweat and sacrifice, living implies risk. And he tells me the story of a woman, freckled like me, with black hair like me, with pale veiny skin, covered in tears. This woman lives in torment, afraid a murderer will break in at midnight and slit her throat. At first any noise makes her uneasy. The crunch of the floor at the foot of the bed, the steps of the insomniac neighbour pacing upstairs, the sounds from the other flats that filter through the paper-thin walls. She can barely get any sleep because after hearing these signs she feels compelled to go to the front door and look through the peephole to make sure no killer is lurking. But that means she is getting up so many times at night that she scarcely stretches out in bed at all. So, one day she decides that she will spend the whole night there, with her eyes glued to the door, to eliminate any trace of doubt. But deep down she knows not even that will ensure she doesn't meet a violent end. The astute psychopath could always come up with a strategy to enter via the balcony, or slide down a rope from the interior patio and come through the window. So the woman stayed up all night, although not even that calmed her apprehension, and the lack of sleep had her trudging through the world all day like a zombie whose throat had been slit.

I am that zombie. 'Why are you so afraid of a murderer when you've already murdered yourself?' And then, to lighten up the session, Jaume says we should sing. He starts improvising a little ditty with a flamenco tinge: 'Ayyy, Mar, she's wishing on a star, to exile death afar, ayyy, Mar,' he croons as he claps his hands. He says that humour is a very good tool in psychology and that I need much more of it. 'All that Euripides and all that Greek tragedy ... What you need is a good rumba.' And we both start singing the tune he's just invented: 'Ayyy, Mar, she can't stop trying to drive the car, ay, Marrrr.' Jaume has managed – despite the fact that I have no rhythm, despite my tone deafness and lack of lustre – to get me singing *bulerías*, and I let out one chortle after the other as I embrace my insignificance and the lightness that could surround me.

'Remember that song,' he says right before I leave. 'You and your children are biological beings subject to the laws of life. Life is not your enemy, because there is no other alternative.'

On my next trip to Madrid I am softly singing that melody we made up and remembering Jaume's warning about the biological reality of my existence and of David and Sara's. I've ignored my materiality all my life, I've rejected it, and now it is taking revenge and bodies float all around me with hypnotic persistence. The bodies of my children, of course, but also those of everyone punished throughout history by laws that, far from being natural, are the result of the most artificial cruelty. Politics confronts me with thousands of bodies: those who've died trying to reach refuge in another land; those who wait years for the right to be taken care of; those who waste away as a number on a waiting list. Mothers have always had a special relationship with bodies, because the weight of protecting them has fallen on us: the angel in the house, precisely because she has the duty of caring for her child, learns that in order to do it well she has to break the domestic bars and burst into public space with a legendary strength everyone insisted oozed from her every pore.

I remember as a little girl, watching that television, with its convex screen and hunched back, in the dining room as dozens of women with white kerchiefs on their heads walked holding candles. When I asked my father who they were, he answered, Argentinian mothers searching for their children.

In the 1970s and 80s, during the military junta's dirty war, the death squads disappeared thousands of young people because of their political ideas. It is estimated that some thirty thousand Argentinians were kidnapped and murdered, but it is hard to give an exact figure because the vast majority of bodies were never recovered. A group of mothers began to gather in the square in front of the presidential residence, the Plaza de Mayo, to demand justice. With carpenters' nails in their hands and a white veil covering their hair, they were Madonnas whose sons had been stolen. The Mater Dolorosa was again personified in our world, but neither the clergy nor the army liked this new version: 'The mothers of the Plaza de Mayo pervert the role of mother ... I cannot imagine the Virgin Mary shouting, protesting, spreading hatred when her son – our son – was taken from her arms,' said a captain. A bishop was even more explicit when he stated that 'the mothers of the Plaza de Mayo have to be eliminated.'

I vividly remember the photographs of their sons that those mothers wore hanging around their necks, with visible faces that made their absence more evident. They also walked with figures of full-size silhouettes. It's difficult to imagine how someone could witness that sight of bodies who are no longer there without feeling a flicker of compassion. But the dictatorial power preferred to say that the mothers were crazy, hysterical, emotional terrorists. Those men, who had used fear to justify to Argentine society the brutal violence with which they implemented their power, were now discrediting the use of sentiment. They didn't censure emotion itself, but merely emotion that was out of their state control, this pain and this rage that the mothers spat into their faces.

Years after my father explained who those mothers were and what the Argentinian dictatorship had done, the Iraq war would activate me politically. Always by his side, I went out onto the streets to shout the 'No to the war' that resounded throughout our cities, and during the catastrophic week of the Jihadist attacks on the Atocha Station we marched to the headquarters of the ruling party, the one that got us into that barren war, and we joined the protests demanding the end of the manipulation, the truth about who had murdered those 192 bodies trapped in the trains.

At that time, another tragically famous mother, Cindy Sheehan, would remind me of the mothers of the Plaza de Mayo. She toured the United States promoting pacifism, with a photo of her son Casey, who died in the first days of the Iraq War. During months she kept vigil in front of the White House, always with the picture of Casey hanging around her neck so everyone would see him. On one occasion she told a journalist that while she was often presented as a mother who had lost her son in Iraq, 'I didn't lose my son. I know where he is. He is buried here [Vacaville]. He was put in a grave by George Bush and the neo-conservatives, a government of psychopathic killers.'

Those words abruptly bring us to that valley of dead bodies and ash that is war, to the bones without tendons and the sheared wool, and all the corporeal and political aspects of motherhood. Sheehan practiced an embodied activism that rejects abstract rationalism and shouts out how politics affects all our children.

At first, public opinion embraced Sheehan as an afflicted mother. But gradually it began to criticise her and label her as crazy, radical. In the struggle for peace, Sheehan transgressed the supposedly rational time limit of grief and the private role of a mother. Sheehan had already cried enough in public and should go back home to take care of her other children and her husband. In the first century, Seneca wrote the text *De Consolatione ad Helviam Matrem* to his mother, in which he tries to console her for his own banishment to Corsica. And the orders he gives her are clear:

> You must not pay regard to certain women whose grief once assumed was only ended by death – you know some who never removed the mourning dress they put on when they lost their sons. Your life was braver from its start and expects more from you: the excuse of being a woman does not apply to one from whom all womanly faults have been absent ... you were never ashamed of your fertility[.]

Seneca and part of twenty-first-century American public opinion were saying the same thing: continue with your task of growing the bones of the living, forget about the dead once and for all, but resign yourself to the fact that one day someone will decide to crush what you are now taking care of. That's what motherhood is.

Things have never been much different on this side of the continent. The discourse about not reopening wounds, or individualising pain, in exchange for a supposed social peace has run through political debates since the end of our last dictatorship. One day, in the middle of a plenary session in Parliament, papers start to rain down. They were tossed by an elderly woman who now looks at us from behind the railing of the gallery. The ushers rush to remove her. I manage to get my hands on one of the papers. It is a photocopy of a handwritten text denouncing the fact that her father, who was shot in the Civil War, still lies in a ditch, and that the failure to carry out the Law of Historical Memory has meant she hasn't be able to give him a proper burial, bring flowers to the grave he deserved, give her pain a resting place.

I and a group of other MPs leave the chamber to find her, through the back, where she was escorted out. She walks with a cane and can barely stand up straight. 'I don't want to die without burying my father,' she tells us. 'I don't have much time.' Then I recall the words spoken by the man who at the time was Secretary General of the conservative party: 'The leftists are stuck in the past, always railing about someone's unmarked gravesite.' And I think that he wouldn't have the courage, that no one would, to tell this woman, curved by the passage of time, that she has no right to her father's corpse, to the green of a cemetery.

One hundred and eleven thousand two hundred and twenty-six. That is the number of the disappeared in Spain from violence resulting from the coup. Many of their family members are still searching for them, like that woman with the cane. As I write this, nearly six years have passed, and a new Law of Historical Memory has just been passed. And during the debate surrounding it, I again heard the old slogan about not reopening wounds. And this time it was the far right who banded together with the conservatives to decide which wounds should be forgotten and who has the legal authority to open them or close them.

In the tragedy *The Suppliants*, Euripides, in his persistence in giving voice to mothers, created a chorus composed fully of them. They are mothers who have just lost their sons, Argive soldiers who have fallen in the war against Thebes, and who cannot bury them because the Theban king has kept their corpses as war booty. These devastated mothers march to Athens and demand that King Theseus help them recover their sons' bodies. Encouraged by his own mother, Theseus agrees and manages to rescue them. When he returns with the corpses, he himself helps the mothers wash them and prepare them for burial. With this gesture, the king puts himself on their level, becoming just another of the mothers and sharing in their grief. In Ancient Greece it was not normal for a man to publicly expose himself in that way to the crude rituals of pain, much less for the king, who had to rule with an iron hand, to do so. In one of the final scenes, a messenger delivers news of Theseus's behaviour to the King of defeated Argos, who exclaims, 'A dreadful burden this, involving some disgrace.' However the messenger replies, 'Why, what disgrace to men are their fellows' sorrows?'

Would all those verbose spokespersons who continue to defend thousands of bodies remaining in ditches be capable of getting down on their knees beside the woman with the cane, helping her to clean her father's body and to bury it, covering his tomb with the justice of memory? Could they become mothers the way Theseus did?

I don't forget about my son's spots. During the days when I'm in Madrid, I have moments where I'm not thinking about them, but on the train home, they return to my mind with twice the power. The more I try not to think about them, the more they grow, like fungus making strange patterns. Until I give in to them and the fungus penetrates deep into my lungs. My efforts and popular wisdom, such as 'try to think of something else, don't obsess over it' do me no good. My mind is at war with itself.

Some years ago, an experiment was carried out at a Scottish university to evaluate our ability to suppress thoughts. A group of volunteers had to memorise forty-eight pairs of words. A few hours later, they were shown the first word and they had to recall the associated one; then they were asked to do the opposite, to prevent the word from entering their conscious thought. The scanner images revealed that there was more brain activity when they tried to avoid the word than when they tried to remember it. It is easier to remember than to forget; much easier to bring your nightmare to the centre of your mind than to an abandoned corner.

On more than one occasion, when I reach the halfway point on my train ride to Barcelona, in that desolate desert, I can't take it any longer and I pounce on my phone. Not so very long ago this wasteland was a fertile valley, filled with streams and springs. But today its harshness reminds me of my mind. It is no place for humans, only for jackals and basilisks. The vines and fig trees were destroyed, the crags collapsed, there are no wells nor any trace of water. All that's left are rocks and thistles that pass beyond the train window at the rate of my accelerated breathing. A breathing that stops when someone picks up on the other side of the line and I again ask for an appointment with the doctor. And also, to the same question, 'what's wrong with your son', I answer: 'he has spots'.

I've already visited this paediatrician three times alone with David. And the same scene always repeated: this weedy Madonna, who *wilts and aches*, covered in wool, who eats the doctor's words as if they were manna from heaven, but who just a few hours later is starving again, because it isn't possible for her to sate herself given the uncertainty of the world.

Jaume explains that there are several types of checking that people like me with obsessive behaviours do, and all of them are a trap. But I have grown fond of one of the most dangerous ones, the secret checking, that you share with no one, because you are aware of the reproachful look they would give you, because you know it would earn you another medal in your competition for top prize in madness. And I mix that checking with the empty checking, with no rational value, because they are questions that have no answer – what will happen to me tomorrow, what will happen to you, what will happen to the world – or they are posed to people who have no more knowledge or information than you. My mother is usually the target of this sort of checking, and the poor woman often answers with the 'I'm not a doctor' that, exhausted, she mumbles after I repeat the same interrogation I apply to medical professionals. I could ask her about quantum mechanics and, a retired office worker, she would be equally obliged to come up with the right answer.

When I can no longer stand the weight of this burden, I confess to my mother that I've been taking David to the doctor in secret and I ask her to come with me to one last visit. I can't process the information, I keep running each sentence over in my mind in an infinite loop, I wear out the doctor, find no comfort, and cannot get out of this black hole that eats up all matter.

We meet up at the health centre. She had gone to my house to pick up David, I was coming straight from Madrid. She waits for me at the entrance and, even from a distance, I believe I can see on David's cheeks, illuminated by the red gleam on the horizon, unusual shapes, colours, islands growing again. The symptoms of my anxiety have been evolving and, recently, at any sign of alarm – before my heartbeat accelerates, my head starts burning, and I become a trembling rag – it shows up in my teeth. I can feel them weakening, about to fall out: my incisors, my canines, my molars. I haven't found a scientific explanation for this sensation that is so real and so dismal. At first I thought it could be an acceleration of my circulatory rhythms, then I thought the opposite; or maybe it was an increase in the temperature of my oral cavity. The doctors I consulted wrinkled their noses, and I had to find a different sort of reasoning: what do I want teeth for when disaster is imminent, who wants to eat at the gates of misfortune? My teeth are wise and react to the force of the world with force. The mills will cease to mill. But my teeth won't fall out. I cling to life like a leech.

My mother tries to calm me, and since my son is there and I fear wounding his subconscious, I quiet myself. Finally we enter the doctor's office. I sit down in a half-broken chair, defeated, and I let my mother be the one to speak with the doctor. And she repeats to her what she told me on my previous visits, that David is fine, that she can't promise he won't have spots in the future, but that he doesn't have them now. 'I don't have a crystal ball, but right now the baby is fine.'

Faced with the pathetic spectacle I've become, my mother tries to justify me, 'My daughter is an MP, she's just concerned.

The twins were premature.' I jab her ribs with a pointy elbow, she lowers her head and stops speaking.

The doctor addresses me for the first time all afternoon. 'You can't do it all, you don't have to control everything, perfection doesn't exist. You don't need to come back, you can trust me.'

I will not visit the doctor again to ask about David's islands. I've been tempted to on many occasions, but when I am in the desert, about to grab my phone, I remember her last words.

11

I end up spending more and more time in Madrid and I feel immensely lonely. I find the city's size overwhelming. I can't seem to orient myself without a sea as a reference point. I have nothing even resembling a home and I go from hotel to hotel, where the asepticness of the room pierces my flesh like a stinger. I don't feel I have the energy to socialise with my new colleagues, and not even calls from old friends who now live in the capital get me out on the streets. I'm afraid that people can see, in the drawing traced by my veins, the obsession that runs through them. Madrid is a city that boils over with community activities and I decide to seek in them the comfort I cannot find anywhere else. In a social centre occupied by squatters, which unfortunately has already been crushed by the weight of real-estate speculation, I join one of the mutual support groups for people with psychic suffering that meets there each week. Made up of ten women with psychiatric diagnoses, we meet in a room furnished with pieces rescued from the street and spend two hours trying to also rescue each other. We talk, making pacts of caretaking and solidarity. And we shake off the stench of madness beneath that flaking ceiling.

The anarchist thinker and naturalist Piotr Kropotkin said that, unlike the too narrow interpretations of Darwinian theories, the evolution of the species is not only explained by mutual struggle, but also by a law of mutual aid. This law is based on an instinct of sociability that developed slowly and taught us that helping each other would make us stronger: it protects us from our enemies' ferocity; it helps us to acquire vital food supplies; it increases our longevity and makes us more perceptive. And to demonstrate this he uses the example of ants: if two ants from the same anthill or colony run into each other and one is hungry, it will ask the other for food and the other will always comply by opening its mouth and expelling substances from its stomach to nourish its comrade. This is such a common action among ants that their digestive organs comprise of two parts: the back is designed for their survival and is devoted to digesting their own food; while the front is for generosity and sharing their daily bread. This solidarity would explain their high mental development, which allows them to build infrastructures as complex as cities filled with skyscrapers, and why they haven't gone extinct despite being, in theory, weak and stunted beings with no shell and a stinger that's pretty useless unless they're in a large group. But Kropotkin maintains that, together, ants are capable of striking terror into insects much larger than them, like crickets, spiders, or beetles, who run away in horror when they see them coming en masse.

I would like to think that we are like that too, gathered here, in this building with broken windows around a butane heater that fails to offer us any warmth. But we don't care. When leaving those group meetings, we are stronger. After practicing my listening and being heard by them, I feel so big that I would swear I could, with a huge stride, place one foot in the Mediterranean and the other in the Manzanares River.

Each one of those women was inspiring for me, and I am aware that, if it weren't for our madness, our widely varied backgrounds mean we would probably never have found each other. I listen, spellbound, to Sara, a poet from El Bierzo of surprising talent who lives in unjust precariousness that plunges her even further into her psychic angst. *My diagnosis has the proportions of a skylight*, I read in one of her poems. Sara manages to write despite medications capable of immersing her in eternal lethargy, despite this madness that nips at her heels. I'm envious of Sara, of her ability to make an impact with words, of the testimony of her suffering she will leave behind. And she doesn't know it because her self-worth is so low. Elisa, a student activist who is unexpectedly clever, explains to us that she tries to scare off her anxiety by painting nails in her spare time. I suggest she paint mine, which seem pale and insipid. She says that, under a magical light she has, she can turn them into precious metals.

In Parliament everything is different. Even though the foundations are much firmer than at the squatters' social centre, there is an atmosphere of oppressive vapours that could cause those robust fireplaces to collapse and all the windows to shatter. I make some friends, but distrust hovers over the parliamentary group. There is something crazy about wanting to be a politician as your calling. Most likely, a classical psychiatrist would say that my entrance into politics contains some delusions of omnipotence: I believed that my actions could change the world, that I could defeat the economic and moral forces that put obstacles in my path. But there is also a component of madness in the ability to remain in politics, unscathed by the party dynamics that can tear you apart in the blink of an eye. Like a blade of grass, you have to be willing to stay unflappable in the face of the highs and lows of drought and rain, that can just as easily seat you on the right hand of the heavens as rip you out by the roots. I don't fare well in this territory: I have no strategy or family to protect me. I understand that politics entails not only pointing out the mistakes of others but admitting to one's own, and I can't deny that I and those around me also err. And that makes me immensely weak in a kingdom where weakness is not considered an opportunity but the worst of sins.

Which is why the mutual aid group sessions are a festival where I flaunt all my fragility. When I am weak, I am strong. I want to make this slogan the needle of my compass, and I try to convince the women around me of it. But some of their stories disprove my words. Some of us have been diagnosed with what are called minor mental illnesses like depression or anxiety, but others live beneath the weight of a label of schizophrenia or bipolar disorder, a hindrance they will never be free of and that has led them to be institutionalised against their will. A woman about fifty years old explains how they left her screaming, tied to a gurney, for an entire night, how she pissed herself, gripped with panic, how she yelled herself hoarse with screams that brought the other patients out of their rooms. Her stories take me back to the Bedlam of my readings, to those Victorian women in straightjackets with shaved heads that wandered through inhospitable rooms. As surprising as it seems, here and now, the same torturous spirit is alive and well in some psychiatric wards.

In Italy, in the 1970s, the psychiatrist Franco Basaglia managed to establish the foundations of a revolution to eliminate asylums. He was an attractive man with lush hair. That grey mop of hair, a somewhat abstracted smile and his constant use of his intellect in the service of altruism reminds me of my father. Basaglia's life is like a novel, like the stories of the mad he treated. At twenty-two years old he was imprisoned for his anti-fascist militancy. He would forever remember that the prison had 'a terrible odour, the scent of death' that he again smelled the first time he set foot in an asylum. He was able to get out thanks to a fake certificate a doctor friend signed, saying that he had a brain tumour. It was a macabre coincidence, as it was precisely that, brain cancer, that would take his life at only fifty-six years old.

Basaglia began his career at the Gorizia psychiatric hospital, near the border with Slovenia, an institution in the middle of nowhere, with a few miserable souls wandering through rooms with bare walls and an unhealthy humidity. But soon psychiatrics from all over the world, journalists, activists, and artists would be drawn to that corner of the planet. Because it was there that Basaglia decided to begin the destruction of the asylum and a change of paradigm from repressive to therapeutic psychiatry. And it all began with a 'No'. He refused to tie up patients, and when they asked him to sign the register of restraints, he answered with a forceful '*e mi non firmo*' – I will not sign – in Venetian dialect. And the hell began to disappear: the bars are eliminated, the doors open, and a community is created based on humane treatment and an understanding of medication as a tool for liberating the individual rather than as another knot.

Years later he would assume the direction of the Trieste psychiatric hospital and becomes world famous without leaving the city thanks to the experiences that took madness beyond those unbearable limits. Like when the patients built a blue horse they named Marco Cavallo, and with it they crossed the walls, like the Trojan horse, to take irrationality outside of the asylum and penetrate the kingdom of reason. Or when in August of 1975 he took a group of one hundred patients on a flight to Venice, in a period when most people had never flown. It was another way to get the mad out of the madhouse, this time in the air. The film director Silvano Agosti recorded the experience in a documentary titled *Il volo*, which shows the patients as initially lethargic, smoking compulsively, and waiting for something to happen. The pilot arrives at the hospital and the patients submit him to a festive interrogation. A woman asks him if she'll be able to look out the window. When the pilot answers yes, she is surprised at this sudden right to glimpse paradise.

In 1977, Basaglia manages to close the Trieste asylum for good. On one of its walls someone writes '*La libertà ès terapeutica.*'

Alongside Basaglia at the Goriza asylum worked another celebrated Italian psychiatrist, Giorgio Antonucci. Antonucci was inspired by Basaglia towards revolutionary thinking and a confidence in the human condition that led him to also say no and to refuse to tie up patients. And I have him to thank for introducing me to the monster of Imola, leaving testimony of her existence.

In 1973, years after working in Goriza, Antonucci started working in the asylum in Imola, near Bologna. There he was in charge of the fearsome Osservanza ward, where they kept the women considered 'incurably agitated schizophrenics'. Before he arrived, the ward was closed and bolted. The walls of the rooms had marks from the fingernails of women who had tried, in vain, to claw their way out. One such room held Teresa B., prostrate in a bed in a straitjacket, held down by straps on her wrists and ankles and wearing some sort of muzzle. She looked like a mummy. She was considered so dangerous that in the asylum no one called her by her name but rather 'the monster of Imola'.

Teresa B. was admitted to that ward when she was twenty-one, right after giving birth to a little girl. According to Antonucci, she was a housewife who also worked the fields and during the postpartum period her performance dropped. That tortured and disturbed her greatly. Her family told the doctor and he sent her without hesitation straight to the asylum, where she was treated with electroshocks. Thirty-three years later, she hadn't set foot outside of it even once.

Antonucci suggests freeing these patients from their shackles. With Teresa he did it slowly and gradually, first one hand and, sometime later, the other. Teresa herself had grown so accustomed to being a threat that she didn't want to be untied. Antonucci gave her more confidence in herself. He even took off the muzzle and managed to get her to stop spitting the way she had before. Her mouth without teeth, which she lost during the electroshock sessions and the feeding by tube, began to trace an incipient smile.

Teresa's medical history prior to Antonucci's arrival reads like those of the Victorian women admitted with the diagnosis of 'puerperal insanity' a century earlier. She arrived at the hospital disturbed and disorientated, fearful. The next day, she remained seated on the bed, seemingly indifferent, and looking towards the door as if waiting for someone to arrive. She responds incoherently to questions and, when reminded of her daughter, shows no emotion.

Just like Emma Riches, she keeps tearing her clothes. In nearly every entry the word 'laceratrice' is repeated, referring to that tendency, for which they decide to keep her tied up almost always. One day she says, laughing, 'I only ripped a dress'; on another, 'what can I do, after ripping clothes I feel good'. Teresa's medical record is a decalogue of defects: 'impulsive', 'dumb', 'dirty', 'disorientated', 'restless', 'dissociated', 'disconnected', 'incoherent', 'with a childish smile'. They label her infantile and accuse her of having an attitude typical of Alice in Wonderland.

When I finish reading the part of her record that is signed by Antonucci, which narrates a progressive improvement, I discover with sadness that Teresa never managed to leave the asylum. Unlike other patients, who returned home with the therapeutic model furthered by the psychiatrist, she stayed in Imola voluntarily. But she could go in and out when she wanted to, stroll through the town, showed joy when receiving visitors. Her daughter hardly ever came to see her.

In 1978, the Italian writer Dacia Maraini interviewed Giorgio Antonucci in Imola. Afterwards she would write a text in which she describes her experience at one of the dances organised in the ward that used to hold the agitated patients. At one point in the evening, a woman asks her to dance. Could it have been Teresa B.? Maraini writes: 'She is short, hardy, with thick, shaggy black hair around a face with strong features. She is missing her front teeth, as are many of the other women; she has bright eyes and an expression of obstinate hilarity that give her a childish air, despite her age.' There is no way to know for sure. Maraini never names the woman, but her description and the words that follow make me think that yes, it is her.

> We dance like two bears, in an awkward and heavy embrace. Later I would learn that this woman was tied up for years and, when the ward was locked, she didn't speak or eat on her own, she spat at anyone who got close to her, and refused clothing and shoes. Now she dances, speaks, eats, walks like anybody else.
>
> Over many years no one thought that perhaps the spitting was a sign of her integrity: instead of turning into a vegetable as the doctors wanted, she obstinately protested, in the only way possible, against her reclusion. Submitted to electroshocks (she received more than fifty), stuffed with drugs, tied hand and foot and with a gag in her mouth, she was objectively an 'idiot'. Now she is again an intelligent person.

I am convinced that woman was Teresa B., and she and Dacia Maraini, dancing to Mozart, directly enter my anthill, and I imagine them often. Alongside Emma, Virginia, Sylvia, and Eliza. And they just keep on coming. Luckily or unluckily, it seems they will never stop coming. There is a whole row of them lined up and on their way, and millions of larvae.

I dance too, at home with my children. When I look back into the past, those first months of motherhood, I think that, despite the anxiety, I was able to convey a bit of tenderness to them. There are certain moments of intimacy in which the fear, while not disappearing, attenuates, and that usually happens when I am rocking them to sleep. The dining room of our home contains an open kitchen with a long granite counter in the centre. When either of the twins can't sleep, I walk around the rock with the baby in my arms and sing a lullaby.

A recurring question in psychiatrists' and psychologists' offices is at what time of day do you feel the worst. I don't know the point of the question, or what my answer implies, but I have always replied without even the slightest hesitation: in the mornings, right when I wake up. It is the first sunlight that reveals the devastated hopes and disasters hidden during the night. The dawn illuminates the smoke that rises off the destroyed city.

When I am in Barcelona, I spend the nights nursing and bottle-feeding, changing nappies, putting David and Sara to sleep again and again, and I can't rest for more than three hours straight. My doctors consider it essential to mitigating my anxiety for me to get what they call restorative sleep. Which is why, in the mornings, my mother or my mother-in-law comes over, or Tomàs is the one who gets up and takes care of the kids in those early hours. Life is already bustling in the dining room when I start to open my eyes. Invariably the first thing I hear is the melody made by a stuffed turtle that we received as a gift when David and Sara were born. When you press it, it plays different children's melodies, all of them placid but catchy and upbeat. However, for me they are the soundtrack of a horror film. Because it is when I hear those melodies that panic overtakes me, the moment when I have to screw up my courage and face up to my children's health by checking that there are no signs for alarm: no spots, my lips don't burn when I kiss their foreheads, there is no whistling in their little lungs. Like that woman who, with the ascending sound of two discordant piano notes, decides to open the closet door to make sure that there isn't a butchering murderer, or that trembling child who looks under the bed in the dead of night to see if there's a monster lying in wait, I would get out of bed and hug my children with a mix of love and anguish. This was the daily routine, and the music of the turtle was its soundtrack. I still have that stuffed animal. I recently changed its batteries, six years later, although my children are already starting to prefer trap to children's songs. Because sometimes I press the turtle's shell and am filled with a burst of memories, as well as the immense guilt and reproaches that I am still dragging around with me for having seen those harmonious melodies as the horrifying sound of destruction. Then my mind spouts apologetic speeches, a thousand apologies to David and Sara. And I remember Emma Riches, how she paced her room in Bedlam, dejected and lamenting having committed some atrocious offense, convinced that she would never be forgiven. And I keep listening to the turtle's music. I think that if I can somehow reconcile myself to it, if I can see its primordial innocence, and not the soot with which I covered it, perhaps I will start to be deserving of that forgiveness.

At night, when I rock the babies to sleep in my arms, everything is different. I sing songs despite having a completely inadequate voice and ear. Tomàs laughs at how off-key

I am, but I don't give up on singing to my children. Then the Apocalypse surrenders to my squawking and sudden joy, and the hills and valleys come alive with me in song. I explain to them, in the five vowels they are starting to articulate, that the sea was salty, salty was the sea. I tell them about that little shark having dinner with his father and mother. I promise them raisins and figs and walnuts and olives, raisins and figs and honey and cheese. And my father, my mother, my grandmothers, and all those songs they would sing, accompany us on those circular walks around the kitchen.

I chose a mutual support group that was all women because I believe there is something in our relationship to madness that unites us. In the Museo de Arqueología in Madrid, a tragic krater – a large vessel for mixing water and wine – shows Heracles's episode of madness, when he threw his son on the pyre. From one corner of the ceramic, the goddess Mania, the personification of insanity and the one responsible for the hero's murderous delirium, looks at him without much surprise. Today the goddess slips through the psychiatrists' offices, where it is mostly us women who are lying on the couches. Eight out of every ten psychiatric pills prescribed are for us. Even the WHO shows, with overwhelming statistics, this asymmetry between the sexes. If we ask doctors and not Greek divinities, they will say that we have risk factors that incline us towards insanity and grief: gender-based violence and sexual abuses, poverty and precariousness, never-ending workdays ... If we ask the women who visit their offices, they will add, from their own experiences, that everything about us is susceptible to being read as madness.

When I entered Parliament, I took a decision: in all of my interventions on the floor, I would speak about two things, women and books. Because gender and literature are so transversal to everything I live and breathe that I'm not able to subtract myself from that imperative. One day when we are debating a non-legislative proposition on mental health, I am chosen to set my group's position in the plenary session. And that day, more than ever, I follow my precept, and I show the percentages of women punished by insanity, and I recite verses of those who had the opportunity to leave testimony. When I finish my speech, an MP in an impeccable suit and tie reproaches my sticking feminism into everything. 'That obsession of yours,' he says to me. I try to argue with him, using scraps of medical and sociological history, with statistics from such diverse sources as the Ministry of Health and the American Psychiatric Association. But he shakes his head and tries to crush me with an arrogant smile. I fantasise about burying him under the thousands of pages of madwomen that I've read, their experiences and complaints, their hopes and tragic endings. And I see the image of his arrogance sinking beneath all that weight while Ophelia's body emerges from the water and comes back to life.

'A document in madness!' That is Ophelia, according to her brother Laertes and Western culture, which has represented, idolised, and idealised her ad nauseum. In contrast to the metaphysical anguish of Hamlet, Ophelia's madness is the essence of femininity: dressed in white, with a long wild mane of hair, adorned with garlands of wildflowers that relate her to ever-changing nature. Ophelia's death in the water is as fluid as the liquids that surround our existence: milk, blood, tears.

So we understand that Ophelia has gone mad, Shakespeare sends us an unequivocal sign: this woman, once so chaste, appears in a scene singing obscene songs that make the Elizabethan audience blush. Centuries later, in Victorian England, the display of explicit sexuality would set off all the alarms within asylums. Many inpatients were accused of masturbation and subjected to constant vigilance. Mrs Wilson, admitted to the Royal Edinburgh Asylum with 'a well marked lactation case', pounced on the doctor or any other man who entered the room, asking them to get into bed with her: 'She says the only thing she needs is a Man & if she cd only get that she wd be all right.' To keep them from consummating their lust, patients like Mrs Wilson were put in leather gloves and tight jackets known as polkas. And an intense debate was begun: the doctors wanted to know if these obscene displays were the pathological result of an organic alteration or the revelation of the women's natural salaciousness that, kept under control in their daily routine, overflowed when madness released the brakes.

For me, on the other hand, since my children were born, sex has disappeared. Because I am so afraid for my body that I'm incapable of touching it or letting anyone else touch it. And because I have so internalised the discourse of guilt that all possible pleasure, especially if it has a corporeal element to it, seems a sacrilege. I have become an extremely chaste woman who is shocked by carnal satisfaction. The summer approaches with giant steps, and I fear it with the same strength with which it will burn me. I don't want to take off my layers of clothing, I don't want nudity and sensuality, I don't want the sea and bristly hair.

There is an Ophelia who sheds the clothing that is sinking her into the stream, an Ophelia who shows her body with no modesty. She is nothing like the Ophelia painted by the Pre-Raphaelite artist John Everett Millais that has lodged itself in our imaginations, the languid Ophelia with her lips parted in eternal silence and her hands outstretched to receive her destiny without resistance. The Ophelia I want defeats death and walks on water, and I have decided that in this summer season that is about to arrive she will be my mirror. I think of that Ophelia who swims, finds the river's surface, and emerges from it. In this Ophelia there is shadow along with light, but this new heroine seems willing to live with them both.

I believe my mother suffered many of the things that make women more susceptible to inhabiting the kingdom of madness. She divorced when I was only two years old and my sister was four. My father had been having an affair with a coworker for some time. He had fallen in love with her, but he didn't leave home. It had to be my mother, who still loved him, who told him he had to go. After they broke up, she was the one who stayed with us, and only every other weekend did she have a break from the constant attention we required. She struggled with a dermatological ailment from the age of six and with the psychological problems that led my teenage sister to lock herself in her room for a whole year. Even though she had family support, her self-sacrificing shoulders had to hold up a thousand daily cave-ins.

She had a steady clerical job and a salary she could live on, but she also suffered economic worries, especially over the security she wanted to leave us if she was no longer around. Once she showed me a file folder with a label where she had solemnly written: 'Open in case of illness or death'. I told her that I didn't want to know anything about that, that it made me anxious. She answered: 'I need you to know where it is.' When I heard the door to the house close, I opened up the file. There was a living will, in which she asked for euthanasia if she was unable to regain consciousness or in pain, and a life insurance policy that named my sister and me as beneficiaries. I know that her doubts over what would happen to us if she were suddenly gone haunted her, and in a way that is still the case.

Olympe de Gouges dared to claim, in the midst of the French Revolution, among shouts of 'egalité, fraternité, et liberté', that women should also have those rights. She wrote the 'Declaration of the Rights of Woman and of the Female Citizen', took pulpits, and published incendiary political texts. She was executed by guillotine. Her last letter, written the night before she was killed, was addressed to her son and, amid the most ardent idealism, she included something very mundane and pragmatic: she reminded him that she had left a watch and some jewellery at the pawnshop. That's something my own mother would have done, up on the gallows, amid the revolutionary fervour and victim of one of the biggest injustices in history. She would have worried about her daughters having dinner that night, and before her head rolled on the ground, she would have asked the executioner to tell us that there is a file folder with an envelope, there, behind the mirror in her room, with a life insurance policy, and that we didn't have to worry about anything.

Despite the obstacles and concerns, my mother always maintained an admirable sanity I would've liked to have inherited. She only succumbed once, when we were very small. Years later she would tell me about it. And even her madness was sweet and somewhat innocent. During just a few weeks she was obsessed by an idea: that the moon was about to fall. And that made her anxious as night fell, when the satellite appeared before her eyes and its presence and risk of falling were inescapable. She got over that obsession in a short time and unscathed, according to her.

I can't imagine life without my mother. And that's even though I left home quite young and have lived in different cities hundreds of kilometres from her. But when I'm nervous, anxious, I still lean on her chest, where I barely fit, and she still strokes my hair, with the smoke from her always lit cigarette blinding me. I think that, in her old age, I am not the support she needs; I think I am still an endless source of worry. During my infertility treatment, I started to have tinnitus. What began as a slight whistle I heard in the mornings, and which I originally attributed to some ambient noise, soon became a chorus of infernal machines that relentlessly assaulted my left ear. After several tests, the ear specialist confirmed that there was no underlying problem: it was my brain that was creating that buzzing, and it had probably been set off by a tense situation. When my mother, always by my side, explained the process I was undergoing, it all made sense. The hypochondria that would run rampant after I gave birth had already started to show its first signs, and there were nights when the persistence of those acoustic daggers defeated me and I would be panicked over going deaf. Then I needed to be with my mother. I would ask her to come over, or I would pack a few things into a bag and go to her place. 'Don't ever die,' I would tell her. As if she could control that. And she would answer, laughing, 'darn, because I was already looking forward to it.'

Once, when I was already in my thirties, after a night of alcohol and sex with a stranger, I was sleeping restlessly. My lover was still beside me. Upset by a nightmare I can no longer recall, I woke up shouting for help: 'Mum! Mum!' I sometimes remember that, with a mix of humour and embarrassment, and I try to imagine what that man (who I've also completely forgotten) must have been thinking. I never saw him again.

In my teenage years, my very atheist parents impassively witnessed my sudden conversion to Christianity. I would read the Bible, the lives of the saints, and the poetry of the mystics. I delighted in the stigmata of Saint Francis of Assisi, in the miracles of the pious Virgin, in the martyrdom of the apostles. I think that this unexpected faith was partly a product of literary fascination but, most of all, a rebellion against my militantly communist family that relentlessly rejected the Church and its God. In those days I already went to my father's house alone every other weekend, and on Fridays and Sundays I would ride the same bus, the number 27. Sitting up at the front, there was often a woman dressed always in black, eccentrically, and with extremely white skin thanks to her powdery makeup that was clearly visible. She would often insult the other passengers, with grunts or expletives. I would avoid looking at her, hoping I'd go unnoticed. But one day our eyes met briefly and she shouted at me, perfectly clearly, 'fucking Christian'. From that day on I felt terrible panic. That diabolical woman was able to read my thoughts. In my mind she was a witch who, part of a coven with others like her, could summon up Satan, or she was a deranged lunatic, my imagination couldn't decide which.

Later I learned that madwomen had suffered the same stigma as witches throughout history. The hysterical, the neurotic, just like the disciples of the devil, provoked chaos. They are impure and they corrupt what they touch. And even though the flames of the Inquisition no longer burn, the rejection and suspicion survive.

When she was old, my grandmother suffered a senile dementia that limited her mobility and forced us to move her into a home. Her roommate, also with dementia, would constantly scream at her: 'witch, witch, witch.' Always three times, like some sort of magic spell. I was little, but I clearly remember the voice and image of that old woman who, like my grandmother, believed she lived in another time and another place. Her daughter explained to me that she had been a seamstress. Every once in a while, when I was close to her, she would grab a hem of my coat and start sewing imaginary stitches, with surprising agility and skill considering her advanced Alzheimer's. She still retained those reflexive movements she'd repeated over thousands of hours under the lights of the tailoring shop. And she also retained that ancestral knowledge that says women who stray from the norm are mad or witches.

In the Middle Ages, one of the tests for determining whether someone was a witch was immersion in freezing water: if the woman floated, she was considered guilty of witchcraft; if she sank, she was innocent. That same water, that same cold, was also used to cure madness.

It was the Flemish doctor Jan Baptist van Helmont who, in the seventeenth century, began to use that therapy after he was told a story. A lunatic had escaped from the asylum, they explained, and jumped into a lake; he was about to die but he managed to get out alive and newly sane. Van Helmont decided then to follow that example, convinced that the water would assuage the ardent madness. He would undress his patients, tie their hands, and stick them headfirst into the water. It seems that some of them drowned, and it seems none of them were cured. But hydrotherapy continued to be practiced in a safer, but not always less violent, way.

In the nineteenth century, Scottish physician Alexander Morison designed a device he called the Douche. It was a sort of container, in the shape of a coffin, into which the patient was introduced with legs and hands bound. Only the head emerged, a collar holding it in place. Psychiatrists of the 1800s were convinced that madness originated in the brain. So the Douche sprayed a constant strong jet of freezing-cold water onto the patient's head.

One of the victims of this torture was a patient of Dr Morison's who suffered puerperal mania. She went by the initials E. E. L., was twenty years old and was admitted twenty days after giving birth to her second child. According to Morison's testimony, the extremely distraught woman insisted she had thousands of children. To cure her, they shaved her head, administered laxatives, and subjected her to more than twenty sessions in the Douche. After that, she recovered.

We still have a portrait of E. E. L. before she went through the wretched device. Dr Morison firmly believed in the science of physiognomy and left behind portraits of his patients beside his notes in their files. In E. E. L.'s we read that, like Emma and Teresa, she ripped her clothes. I wonder why they all did that despite knowing they would be tied up, and I think that might be precisely the reason.

The Dominicans who wrote the most influential book on witch-hunting, the *Malleus Maleficarum*, had already warned of the difficulty in distinguishing witches from madwomen. Which led to some doctors giving indications to the Inquisitors so they could more reliably perform their jobs. One of the conclusive marks that identified the disciples of Satan was a third nipple, used to feed the beast and his minions. It was not easy to locate, they said, and required stripping the suspect naked and studying every inch of her skin. Where could that woman on the bus be hiding her third nipple, beneath that immense black mortuary shroud she swathed herself in? And what I find even more intriguing, now with these two little leeches who want to suckle every few hours: would she have enough milk to feed an entire legion of demons?

In the same period when Alexander Morison was immersing the mad in freezing-cold water, the celebrated French psychiatrist Philippe Pinel – inspired by revolutionary ideas – tried to break the chains that bound the patients in the Parisian hospitals of the Salpêtrière and Bicêtre and to treat them more humanely. Pinel was, above all, a scientist searching to reproduce in psychiatry the same techniques of observation that had been applied by naturalists. In order to do so, he wandered through the hospital rooms jotting down in a notebook what kind of mental illness each patient had and the criteria to differentiate them: there were those driven mad by love, by domestic strife, and by the events of the Revolution. What label would he give my madness?

Jaume calls it 'disorder of interference by the Grim Reaper'. He prescribes surrender. 'Make use of that verb, which is undervalued but actually quite lovely,' he suggests. I defied nature by giving birth without Fallopian tubes; I came out of nowhere as a candidate promoting justice and love; how could I surrender? It doesn't seem possible. But thanks to my dialogues with him, I am increasingly able to glimpse the beauty he swears is in the act of surrendering. What Jaume recommends for me is a therapeutic surrender, that I be aware of the fact that the more I struggle against uncertainty the more acute my problem becomes. Surrendering is not passivity, it is good sense, Jaume assures me. 'Surrender like we all have,' he tells me, with a smile, 'instead of being a pioneer, in this you're one of the last.'

Pinel sought to bring to psychiatry the same humanity that Jaume is now able to employ with me as he refuses to settle for the pills that the doctors occasionally prescribed.

In his famous *Traité médico-philosophique sur l'aliénation mentale*, Pinel contradicted all those doctors who asserted that insanity comes from incurable brain lesions and that, as such, the only fate for the insane was reclusion and brutality. For Pinel, that inhumane treatment was comparable to the oppression of citizens by authoritarian governments. He was convinced that the treatments had to be focussed on recognising in the patients an overly impassioned sensibility, a quality whose value had to be pointed out and that was often a reflection of the impassioned time period they were destined to live through.

Pinel has become a legend and, beyond the debates about psychiatric history, the image of him freeing the mad maintains its place in the collective imagination, as immortalised by Tony Robert-Fleury in the painting that still hangs in the Salpêtrière. The French psychiatrist is in the centre, supervising as they remove the shackles from a pretty lady. Another one, grateful, kisses his hand. The rest of the patients, all women, gather on the margins with mournful expressions as they await release from their chains. One lies on her back, imprisoned by melancholy; another gesticulates in an attack of hysteria. Around Pinel crowd well-dressed men, presumably physicians or officials, in representation of reason.

According to documents of the period, Pinel first took the chains off the male patients, and only a few weeks later did he do so with the women. But after Pinel's death, Robert-Fleury, with the support of historical tradition, decided what image of madness should become a symbol recorded for posterity.

I went on a pilgrimage to see the painting. There is a whole geography of madness I pay homage to in each city I visit. There are sites of collective madness, where lunatics of the past once resided, and where I search for their remains like an archaeologist at a dig site. And then there are the sites of individual madness, those where only I know the degree of suffering they've witnessed. There is that maternity ward where I went mad, that bench on a side street by my house where I take refuge to tremble so neither my children nor their father will see me, those toilets in Parliament with gleaming tiles where I cry when no one can hear me, or the single hotel rooms where the only consolation I find during anxiety attacks is on the other side of a telephone line. Barcelona and Madrid are two cities filled to the brim with traces of my madness and while I embrace the possibility of surrender that Jaume offers me, I am also learning to reconcile myself with their scarred streets.

12

Sara and David are extremely different. It is surprising that, having received the same stimuli since they were just a yearning, they've evolved in such an oblique way. And I am mesmerised watching the directions they take, so unique to them and which science is far from being able to explain. I see them as if in a painting by Sorolla, with a light whose origin I cannot pinpoint but that illuminates a concrete area each time and forces me to squint. Sara's mouth, even in a neutral position, traces a slight upward arc that, when she furrows her brows, gives her a pensive air. She's put on weight and her rounded body now sits tall upon the pillars that are her buttocks. From that position, she analyses her surroundings, undaunted. With her almond-shaped eyes she seems to want to control everything, as if judging us with a placid child's wisdom, which has already been able to forget how she was gasping for breath not so long ago. She has a turned-up nose and huge chubby cheeks. The three things form a perfect triangle and they are the buoys I cling to millions of times during the long days of domestic life. David, on the other hand, smiles with a generous mouth. His nose, larger than his sister's, is the tower that surveys bright and slightly bulging eyes that seem to be ready for adventure. Everything about him is mayhem and sensitivity. He often suffers from reflux and before expelling the milk from his mouth or nostrils, he wriggles like a tadpole searching for the surface. And then he explodes into boisterous crying. I run from wherever I am in the house to pick him up and he curls around my body like a tendril seeking comfort. It's okay, just a little bit of milk, and I am a flowing source of plenty. I lie to him. For a while now, my breasts have been producing little, because of my anxiety, or my trips to Madrid, who knows.

But if there is something that sets the twins apart from each other, the first thing that strangers notice and comment on, it's the colour of their eyes. Sara's are a glowing, aquamarine blue. David's are very dark, two black flames in contrast with the white of his sclerae. The perfect circles of my children's irises are my magical amulets, which I need and proudly flaunt, but they have a very mysterious power that fills me with apprehension.

At birth, the retina isn't completely developed. In fact, sight is the least realised sense in babies. And in the case of preemies, that is even more true. Although no one is able to tell me how long exactly, David and Sara will take longer than other babies their age to see clearly. It is very likely they will have myopia, hyperopia, astigmatism, and endless other things whose names I don't even fully comprehend. Every childrearing manual explains clearly what babies see: at first, just blurry shadows in greyscale; at three months they can already make out primary colours; by five months they recognise familiar faces; and at six they can perceive depth and all sorts of colours. I, on the other hand, don't know what my children can see. And to figure it out I undertake strange rituals with their gazes. I enter and leave their fields of vision to check whether they follow me with their eyes, I draw closer and back, I place a hand in front of them and shake it anarchically, I jump and dance around the room. I make myself laugh imagining what someone would think if they were peeking in at me. That madwoman. That madwoman who is a mother and an MP. Two babies and a country in her hands. Those are moments of laughter and uproar, of anxiety that overflows into play, and I hope they also remain in their unconscious, and that one day they can recall them.

David and Sara are already almost six months old and it's time for their checkup at the paediatrician's. I show up with a long list of questions; Tomàs resigns himself and lets me ask them all, even though this time I manage to do it without my usual desperation. During the visit, the doctor points out the size of Sara's pupils. They are very small, she says, and starts to move the otoscope, that instrument similar to a torch that is used to examine ears. She directs the ray of light onto one of Sara's eyes, bringing it closer and back again. 'Look', she says to us. Her father and I rush over to see how her pupil grows smaller when the otoscope is very close to it, a dot in the immensity of the sea. Because of her prematurity, and this tininess that we hadn't noticed until now, the doctor schedules a visit with the ophthalmologist. We dress the babies and leave the office. Except for that one detail, everything went well, they're perfect, gaining weight and height. Before we go, the paediatrician prints out that routine chart for every parent of a preemie. Their line is ascendent. In this race that is growing up, even though we know they won't be among the leaders, they are starting to approach the large group in the middle that indicates normality. And that word sounds so good coming out of a doctor's mouth.

When we get home I look at Sara's pupils. That tiny black circumference that could scarcely be seen at the paediatrician's is now, in the darkness of the room, bigger than ever. The Greek philosopher Empedocles claimed that blue eyes were due to an abundance of heat. That's why blue-eyed people can see in the dark, because the fire in their eyes lights up the darkest spaces. I'm surprised to catch myself thinking that there is nothing wrong with those two burning stars that are now Sara's pupils. And I smile as I confirm, with my gaze running over the bodies of my children in their cribs, their prodigious growth, the miracle of the normalcy of their weight and size, their habits and gestures.

When I take Sara to the oculist a few days later, they put drops in her eyes to dilate her pupils and examine them more clearly. They send us to the waiting room for half an hour while the drops take effect. During that time, I watch carefully as Sara's pupils slowly dilate, as if wanting to eat up the blue of her irises. Land stealing territory from the ocean. Her eyes are watery, and every so often a tear slips out. Then, as if by mimesis, another springs up in mine.

I once read that the chemical composition of tears varies slightly depending on what motivates them and what part of the brain is involved in their production. I wonder what the tears of a mother are made of. And the first thing that comes to my mind is from history.

The quintessential maternal tears are those of the Virgin Mary, who not only cries for the death of her son, but for all of humanity. Mothers have always been the best at crying, and we have a good model: every one of Mary's tears is a mirror that reflects ours. And Mary cries with tenacity, subverting even the laws of physics; Mary cries to the point of miracle. Like the Madonna delle Lacrime, who, sculpted in plaster, shed tears for four days and four nights from the walls of the home of a modest Sicilian couple in 1954. The wife, pregnant and suffering from preeclampsia, went blind and sought refuge in prayer. One day she suddenly recovered her sight, just at the precise moment a transparent liquid began to stream down the cheek of the effigy of the Virgin in her dining room. Hundreds of people were drawn to her home, neighbours, clerics, and a commission of doctors, who affirmed the human origin of the tears. A local cameraman filmed the marvellous occurrence, and still today there are more than three hundred stills of the crying. The video can be seen on YouTube, and to me the tears seem very big, out of proportion with the size of her eyes. But I suppose that there is a hierarchy even in tears, and hers encompass an entire world.

The philosopher Julia Kristeva describes how in the representations of the Virgin Mary motherhood is expressed through tears and milk, and that both are metaphors of nonspeech. As mothers we are denied language, and only have these two fluids with which to call out to the world. My milk stopped flowing two weeks ago and all the liquid that doesn't spring from my nipples floods my tear ducts. Since I became a mother I cry constantly, over everything, sometimes over nothing. It worries Tomàs, and he always asks me not to cry in front of the children. He thinks that I might scar them with my pain, and his hesitations seem reasonable to me. So I try to cry where no one can see me, in some corner of a small flat that has very few. Weepers, to the back of the closet.

But mothers' tears flood the earth. That happens at daybreak, when drops of crystalline water settle on the leaves of the geraniums on my terrace. They are the tears of Eos, the goddess of the dawn. Every day, she rises from her bed in the east, gets into a chariot and heads to Olympus, where she announces the arrival of her brother Helios. One of her four children, Memnon, died by Achilles' hand in the Trojan War. Eos still cries for him, and it is the fruit of her grief that meteorologists insist on calling dew.

Memnon also cries for his mother, or that's what Greek travellers to the necropolis of Luxor thought when they recognised him in one of the two colossi at the temple of Amenhotep III. In the mornings, just at dawn, this giant statue gave off a sort of moan, a melodious wail they interpreted as a son's greeting when he felt the touch of his mother, the dawn. Not long ago, one of the colossi was restored, and Miguel Ángel López Marcos, a specialist stone conservator and head of the project, offered a scientific explanation for the phenomenon. The sound was a creaking produced by a crack in the quartzite from an earthquake. The stone made the noise when it expanded due to the temperature variances in the desert between night and day, sometimes as much as forty degrees. The crack continued expanding and no longer gives off any sound. That colossus also does not represent Eos's son, but the pharaoh Amenhotep III, to whom the temple is dedicated. There is no wail. There is no reunion between mother and son at dawn. There are only minerals that expand and condensation from the air's humidity. And mothers crying, hidden.

The ophthalmologist determines that there is no problem with Sara's vision, although he says we should follow up on it because of her prematurity. When we get home after that tearfulness shared between mother and daughter, our cheeks still salty, David is playing on the dining room rug. He turns his head and smiles at us with that enormous mouth. Sara and I smile back at him. I take her out of the pram and place her beside him. And they begin to swim on land, lifting their heads with effort, trying to keep them nice and straight, like two clumsy tightrope walkers. They laugh among themselves. I walk over to them. And I would say that David is trying to caress us, wipe away our tears, with those arms and hands that are still tiny but perhaps already have the instinct to comfort. His lively eyes are like those of a heron willing to gobble up any snake of pain.

In the Middle Ages an iconography of a different Madonna emerged, not widespread but more transcendent than the conclusions of any Council. Inspired by byzantine Virgins, they showed not only the mother caring for her son, but a reciprocal action. The Florentine artist Cimabue painted with tempera and gold, in the Collegiata dei Santi Lorenzo e Leonardo, a Mary who looks out into the abyss, likely aware of the dangers threatening her little one, and a Jesus who touches her cheek to mitigate her suffering.

To contemporary eyes, the scene's tranquillity is broken by the strange figure of the boy, more like a cranky old man than a newborn messiah with all the magnificence and purity of a God. Two theories try to explain the abundance of these aged messiahs in medieval churches. On one hand, it could be due to the lack of skill in their creators, who in a society that doesn't yet consider childhood pertinent enough to be represented in art, had no references and settled for drawing miniature old men. But it is also likely that they were influenced by theologians who declared that Christ was born a fully formed man, and that his mother would have been holding a body with teeth, long nails, and a lush mane of hair. What I find most unsettling about that Christ is his receding hairline that suggests, unlike the images we've been given, he will go to the cross without a single hair on his head. I read somewhere that in that period baldness was considered a sign of wisdom, and in that gesture of comforting his mother this Jesus shows how deeply wise he is.

I sit on the sofa, exhausted from the tension of the visit to Sara's oculist, and I leave the children there, on the floor, moving like joyful worms, exchanging glances. Perhaps I haven't been capable of being the mother I would have liked to be but – no credit to me – I've given them the best gift: each other. Over time they will show the same wisdom of that old baby Jesus in the way they treat one another. In a few months, Sara will say 'David' for the first time, and that moment will remain branded into my brain much more than when she said 'mama'. At little over a year old, David will cut himself on a sharp toy, bleed a little, and Sara will stroke his head. When they can barely speak, every time Sara cries, David will tell her 'it's okay'. And on their first day of school, as I head off and leave them in a classroom filled with strangers, I'll see how they hold hands.

In the years to come, those interwoven hands will be their most stable reference point in a changeable world, in routines that invariably move between two houses. Because one evening when we can no longer avoid the conversation, when Sara and David are little more than six months old, Tomàs and I finally speak the word 'separation'. With a civility that surprises me, we verbalise what we've known for some time already and, with a 'for the good of the children', we take the decision to stop arguing. At first we continue with a forced cohabitation 'for practical reasons', but it ends up flooded by outrage over knowing that this presence will soon be an absence. Even though we continue with everyday life as if nothing has changed, now I know that in the not-so-distant future he will leave, and I will have to renounce conjugating love with an admiration that has colonised my every last cell. For me Tomàs was and is a brilliant man, with sharp perceptiveness, quick wit always at the ready, an intellectual well I could have bathed in my whole life.

Finally, the day will arrive that he moves out and into his mother's house, and a couple of months later, when he has already found a flat, he will tell me he's coming over to take one of the bookshelves and some other things. I will go to a nearby bar so I won't have to witness the crumbling of our home, of our nuclear family, of what I had wanted to be and didn't manage to pull off. I will order a coffee, and while I drink it, I will feel one of the most profound pains I've ever experienced. My library will be split up. Because love, as Sylvia Plath says, doesn't respond to any theory, and the failure of mine with Tomàs's will be, for me, the definitive end of all theories.

During the weeks before Tomàs has his own place, I will take care of the children. Despite his visits and constant attention, despite the support of my mother and my sister, that will be a time of loneliness. And most of all a time of silence, of the phone that doesn't ring, of Tomàs's family who will forget me as if I were dead, of my friends who will flee the headache that a single mother with outbreaks of sadness entails. But, just like Plath, I will idle away that bitterness with walks. Every corner of Barcelona, every park, every square, will see me walking with the heavy double pram, laughing, hugging. I will take them to the zoo, I will tell them a thousand stories and we will solve the puzzles of a separated mother's routine with all the cleverness of a dragon with three heads. And, like the poet, at night I will also prepare milk for my children, but I will manage to wake up in the morning to clean up the remains while I observe their frank smiles. And I will tell myself, as I shake a fabric ball in front of their open eyes to cheer them, and me, up:

Such queer moons we live with
Instead of dead furniture!

I often think there must be something I can use in the thick shrubs of fear I've been cultivating over all these months, something that can be recycled in this summer comeback that has me so hopeful. Couldn't I take all these tears I've saved up in a jar, in an exercise as egotistical as it is submissive, and use them in a book?

When the poet Anne Sexton tried to commit suicide, her psychiatrist visited her at the hospital and said: 'You can't kill yourself, you have something to give. Why, if people read your poems ... they would think, "There's somebody else like me!" They wouldn't feel alone.' Years later, the poet would admit that those words made her feel she had found a purpose for her existence. And yes, there are others like Anne, including me, who have recognised ourselves in her poetry, and found guilt and forgiveness in it, and discovered the treasure that a tortured life leaves behind.

Like me, Anne Sexton was diagnosed with postpartum mental health problems. They began shortly after the birth of her second daughter, Joy, and when the first, Linda, was only two years old. Anne remembered the exact moment when everything shattered.

> I came home late and heard Joy choking, like a dog barking. She couldn't breathe! I ran in and turned on the shower, then spent the whole night in the bathroom with her, thinking she was going to die.

Ever since then, and despite the fact that Joy recovered, Anne lived with a persistent fear that something bad would happen to her daughters, and that set off serious anxiety crises. I recognise myself in her: in that unforgettable scene that would scar her forever, of her baby unable to breathe; in that anxiety that increased in parallel to her maternal responsibilities; in the certainty that as a mother she was unable to keep thorns from pricking the sides of her little ones.

To read Anne Sexton's poetry is to have a conversation with her about motherhood. But about a guilty motherhood, tinged with regret, that inflicts violence and pleads for forgiveness. Writing about being a mother in the 1950s was in and of itself a subversive act, but confessing as she did that motherhood was a source of anguish, while linking mental collapse and suicide attempts to her role as a mother, was extremely radical. The cry that is her poetry is more political than many of the speeches I listen to from my seat in the chamber.

After one of her stints in the madhouse, when her daughters were one and three years old, Anne's family decided she couldn't care for them and sent them to live with relatives. A year later, when Anne had regained some of her lost sanity, the girls would return home, but the guilt would never leave her. Guilt torturing the mother, constantly tripping her up, an obstacle she can never elude. Years later she would dedicate a poem to Joy, 'A Little Uncomplicated Hymn', that strove to be the perfect song to redeem all her sins as a mother.

> A song for your kneebones,
> a song for your ribs,
> those delicate trees that bury your heart;
> a song for your bookshelf
> where twenty hand-blown ducks sit in a Venetian row;

But, at the end of the poem, she herself acknowledges her failure:

> I wanted to write such a poem
> with such musics, such guitars going;
> I tried at the teeth of sound
> to draw up such legions of noise;
> I tried at the breakwater to catch the star off each ship;
> and at the closing of hands
> I looked for their houses
> and silences.
> I found just one.
>
> you were mine
> and I lent you out.
>
> I look for uncomplicated hymns
> but love has none.

In a way I feel that, with this anti-climactic conclusion, Anne Sexton is telling me that, if I want to get out of the pit she sank into, the first thing I must do is accept that, in poetry, like in this form of love that is motherhood, complete success does not exist.

I landed on softer ground than Anne did, and in part it is made up of her deathbed and those of all the mad mothers who preceded me. I see those dead women during this hot month of June, big and small, standing before the throne I've built for them. I open their books and, with their strength, another book opens.

We madwomen have always sung and recited verses. Ophelia, distributing flowers and herbs, sang obscene and melancholy ballads beside the river. As did many of the Victorian ladies who went mad after giving birth. This is how it was enthusiastically described by the nineteenth-century German obstetrician J. F. Osiander, who left testimony of the extreme mania of one of his patients who couldn't stop creating with language: 'This senseless talking and rhyming continued for hours, without a moment's pause. Even when her mouth was held shut, with medicine inside, she continued to murmur.' Another patient invented romantic verses, and Osiander recognised in them 'a surprisingly beautiful and profound quality'.

I too gradually find a bit of comfort and direction in lyrical excess. But I wonder who will care about the tears of a mother in a world so accustomed to considering them redundant.

In 2002, the Giotto frescos in Padua's Scrovegni Chapel were restored. This great masterwork of universal art, hidden inside a modest chapel, was damaged by the salts and other materials that the passing centuries had left on its surface. The characters that make up the scenes from the life of Jesus painted by Giotto on either side of the chapel, their majesty and humanity, were threatened by the corrosion of time. The starry sky of the vault is of that blue tone only Giotto was able to create. Which is why they carried out one of the most ambitious and risky restoration projects ever undertaken, and that epic feat revealed a treasure. In the Biblical scene that illustrates the massacre of the innocents by Herod, the restorers, when eliminating the buildup of history's layers, discovered the tears, hidden for centuries, that ran down the cheeks of the mothers who had just lost their children. In an era when tears were exclusively religious subject matter, Giotto decided to depict these women crying over children who weren't gods. They are small tears that leave a thin trail on the devastated faces of those mothers. They are nothing like the size of those of the plaster Virgin who cries undaunted in Sicily. But their force makes your blood run cold. Although not everyone agrees with that. The restoration was not without its controversy, and many people pointed out the harm it could cause the frescos. That was the view of ArtWatch International, an organisation whose objective is to oversee proper restoration practices and which was vehemently opposed to the project of the Cappella degli Scrovegni. 'Who cares about those mothers' tears?' said Ornella Livigni, one of their spokespersons.

And perhaps she was right. Furthermore, I am afraid to reveal what I've seen inside my mind, to expose all that darkness to the light of day. The Victorian psychiatrist W. W. Godding, concerned about the stigma of madness, advised families not to hospitalise women who were suffering from puerperal insanity: 'Though the recovery is rapid, still she has been insane and this is never forgotten by her friends or her children,' he wrote, 'henceforward there is a certain dread of what may be in the future, a skeleton in the closet, not mentioned but always there.' I know that this book I am starting to imagine will be my skeleton in the closet, and probably also my children's. But I also think that in a way I've incurred a debt. The strength I've found to face up to this summer is thanks to the written word. I feel I also have the duty to raise my voice, even if it's with less virtuosity. I'd like to think that David and Sara are nodding their heads, that they will understand that I felt the need to form part of this chorus. And that in some way I am paying homage to them, to them and to their growing voices, which I want them to let sound out, at the top of their lungs, in the future.

On Midsummer Night's Eve, I arrive home after dark. I am returning from Madrid with news. The negotiations to form a government have failed and there will be a new election. I've taken the decision to run, and stubbornly continue to try to change what many consider immutable. When I walk through the door, I see that David and Sara are waiting for me, sitting up nearly straight, on the sofa. Behind them, through the immense terrace window, I can see the sky, a sea of burning glass where fireworks are bursting. Those lights, like my children's bodies, contain all the colours of the universe. I throw down my suitcase in the entryway and walk over to them. I hug and kiss them while their heads seem to sustain all those shooting stars that announce the solstice. Outside there are the same cliffs and precipices, but in the face of that spectacle I manage to not let them control my thoughts.

Upon seeing me, and receiving my caresses and exclamations, David and Sara start babbling and emitting euphoric shrieks that sound like a thousand trumpets. I solemnly pretend to steal their noses and replace them, pretend to gobble up their toes and then put them back in place, and disappear behind my hand only to become visible again by the art of magic. Over time, first on all fours and later standing, David and Sara will take the lead in our games. They'll furtively seek me out in my room while I'm working and try to surprise me, as if I hadn't heard their sonorous laughter or seen their heads peeking through the doorway. When I arrive home from Madrid, they hide behind a chair or a curtain, very still, unaware that half their bodies are visible; I pretend I can't find them, and they are proud of their skill at hiding.

There is a rule I must obey in these games: I must act as if I haven't seen them, as if I haven't heard their poorly stifled giggles, and thus put the desire for their happiness above the evidence.

That night, sitting by their side, I contemplate how the sky cyclically lightens and darkens. I feel their heat like two lit firebrands on either side. I sing them to sleep and, as slumber overtakes them, my eyes also droop. I dream that a wolf is living with a lamb, that a panther lies down with a kid goat, that a calf and a lion break bread together, and that it is a little boy and a little girl who lead them.

ACKNOWLEDGMENTS

I want to thank all those who try to preserve the memory and testimonies of mad men and women throughout history.

Thanks also to the health professionals who humanely treat physic suffering. In my case, I was lucky to come across Jacobo Chamorro López, Doctor Udina, Doctor Parramón, Doctor Alamán, Doctor Vilarassa, Doctor Roa, Doctor Jordán, and the entire medical team at Parliament.

Many thanks to all those who work in Parliament, especially those in the library and the stenography pool, Roser Comellas and Anna Flotats, and Laura Pérez Castaño, for their support over these years, which weren't completely lonely.

My editors, Mireia Lite and Carme Riera, and their entire team, believed in this book from the beginning and gave me the strength to publish it despite my fears. I'm indebted to the sensibility of Rita Puig-Serra and the singularity of Antonina Obrador for the cover photo.

Patrícia Valero and Laura Gamundí gave me wise advice, and helped me throughout the whole process, in our legendary coven meetings.

I'd like to thank Sara R. Gallardo for being my comrade in madness and lending me her lovely verses from the poetry collection *Ex Vivo*.

I couldn't have written a single word without Telmo Moreno Lanaspa, Alberto Fernández Camino, Montserrat Puig Bassols, Àngels Oliver Bilbao, Cristina Hernández, my sisters Georgina and Irene and my brother Víctor. To them I want to express my thanks but also my regret for any pain I caused them on this journey.

BIBLIOGRAPHIC NOTE AND ACKNOWLEDGMENTS

First and foremost, I want to thank booksellers for their valuable work. I would lose myself in the shelves they curate, and I found true pearls and followed unexpected paths that led me to write these pages. Second-hand booksellers deserve special mention, for providing me with out-of-print volumes that were impossible to find in libraries, rarities that were a fundamental part of the construction of this book. The role of archives in the conservation and diffusion of the first-person history of madness is crucial. I want to particularly thank the archivists of the former Bedlam asylum, now the Bethlem Museum of the Mind, for their help in reconstructing the lives of some of the women who appear in this book.

Many authors before me have investigated the madwomen of the past. The work of Hilary Marland, author of *Dangerous Motherhood*, and Elaine Showalter, author of *The Female Malady*, on the madness of Victorian women was fundamental to this book (as well as my life in recent years). Other books that vindicate the voices of silenced and alienated women are *Mad, Bad and Sad* by Lisa Appignanesi; *Women and Madness* by Phyllis Chesler; *Complaints & Disorders* by Barbara Ehrenreich and Deirdre English, and *Lost Souls* by Diana Peschier. Most of these books are very difficult to find, especially in Spain. I hope they don't ever disappear completely, because an extremely important part of our history would be lost with them.

Reading works that reflect on mental health from a philosophical and historiographic perspective can contribute to a necessary enrichment of our discourse around psychic suffering, and perhaps be more useful to us in difficult moments than the arsenal of self-help books that are published. Some of the books I kept closest to me as I was writing this one are *Histoire du mal de vivre* by Georges Minois; *Madness, A Brief History* by Roy Porter; *Madness and Civilization* by Andrew Scull; *La melancolía moderna* by Roger Bartra; *Hypochondria* by Susan Baur; *Melancholie van de onrust* [Melancholy in Times of Turmoil] by Joke J. Harmsen, and, of course, the monumental *Anatomy of Melancholy* by Robert Burton. Part of the information on the history of psychopharmaceuticals is taken from *Farmacología y endocrinologia del comportamiento* by Diego Redolar Ripoll.

Various books that offer critical perspectives on psychiatry and the official history of madness are also present in these pages, such as *Histoire de la folie à l'âge classique* by Michel Foucault; *L'istituzione negata* by Franco Basaglia (which I read in a translation by Florencia Molina y Vedia); *Il pregiudizio psichiatrico* by Giorgio Antonucci; *Las metamorfosis de la psiquiatría* by Piero Cipriano (in a translation by Giuseppe Maio); *The Divided Self* by R. D. Laing; *Soul Machine* by George Makari, and *La folle histoire des idées folles en psychiatrie*, edited by Boris Cyrulnik and Patrick Lemoine.

It is practically impossible for me to cite all the books and texts I've read on motherhood. However I want to mention some of those that were most important to me, and helped me to get past the stigma that often surrounds this subject and reclaim its universality beyond the gender of the readers or their identity as mothers: *Of Woman Born* by Adrienne Rich; *Mothers* by Jacqueline Rose; *Maternal Thinking* by Sara Ruddick; *A Potent Spell* by Janna Malamud Smith;

Mothers Who Deliver, edited by Jocelyn Fenton Stitt and Pegeen Reichert; *Il bambino della notte* by Silvia Vegetti Finzi (translation by Pepa Linares); *Histoire des mères et de maternité en Occident* by Yvonne Knibiehler; *L'histoire des mères du Moyen âge à nos jours* by Yvonne Knibiehler and Catherine Fouquet, and *Mother of all Myths* by Aminatta Forna.

There are ideas in these pages about women's place throughout history that were influenced by such varied books as *Histoire des femmes en Occident* (in four volumes), edited by Georges Duby and Michelle Perrot (translation by Marco Aurelio Galmarini); *Soror. Mujeres en Roma* by Patricia González Gutiérrez; *A Cabinet of Greek Curiosities* by James C. McKeown; *Women in Ancient Egypt* by Gay Robins, and *Leyendas de la Diosa Madre* by Pedro Ceinos Arcones. Michelle Roche Rodríguez's book *Madre mía que estás en el mito* was one of my most valuable tools for reflecting on the cultural weight of the Virgin Mary.

I want to acknowledge Clare Carlisle, author of *Philosopher of the Heart*, for illuminating me on the love life of Søren Kierkegaard; the philosopher Adriana Cavarero, for making me see Leonardo's work with new eyes, after reading her *Inclinations. A Critique of Rectitude* (in the translation by Anna Carreras i Aubets); Ferran Aisa for vindicating the role of women in the history of class struggle and offering us the words of Amàlia Alegre.

Finally, I owe special gratitude to the translators of the versions I quoted in this book. The words of Marcel Proust from *The Guermantes Way* are in C. K. Scott-Moncrieff's translation, while his letters were translated by Terence Kilmartin. The translation of Seneca is by C.D.N. Costa. The quotations from several of Euripides's tragedies are translated by E. P. Coleridge, in the case of *Hecuba*, *The Trojan Women*, and *The Suppliants* and David Kovacs in the case of *Medea*. Dante Alighieri appears in Courtney Langdon's translation, Kaethe Kollwitz in Richard and Clara Winston's, Roland Barthes in Richard Howard's, Verdaguer in Ronald Puppo's.

IMAGE CREDITS

p. 56: Henry Hering, *Portrait of Emma Riches*, 1857, © Bethlem Royal Hospital Archives and Museum, © AGE

p. 58: Henry Hering, *Portrait of Emma Riches*, 1858, © Bethlem Royal Hospital Archives and Museum, © AGE

p. 104: Telmo Braun, *Portrait of E.M.G.*, drawing on paper, 2016